AUDREY'S WINDOW

by

B.J. BROOKS

Many Blessings
B.J. Brooks
Eph 3:20

CYNTOMEDIA CORPORATION

Pittsburgh, PA

ISBN #1-56315-301-7

Paperback Fiction
© Copyright 2004 Barbara J. Brooks
All Rights Reserved
First Printing — 2004
Library of Congress #2002113711

Request for information should be addressed to:

SterlingHouse Publisher, Inc.
7436 Washington Avenue
Pittsburgh, PA 15218
www.sterlinghousepublisher.com

SterlingHouse Publisher, Inc. is a company
of the CyntoMedia Corporation.

Book Designer: Beth Buckholtz
Cover Design: Melissa G. Hudak — SterlingHouse Publisher, Inc.

Printed in Canada

ACKNOWLEDGEMENT

For my sister Marie who never gave up on my abilities to write.

Her encouragement has helped make a dream come true.

My friend Donna who can make a drab day become sunny.

My friend Mary who pushed me out the door one more time.

PROLOGUE

Fall 1928

The water was cool, clear, and bordering on cold, as well it should since September was nearing its last days. Actually the creek was always cold, but Audrey didn't mind. She was too busy talking to her cousin Estelle to notice the temperature in or out of the water. In reality, it was a beautiful Indian summer day with just a hint of fall in the air.

The creek was a natural divider between their families' properties. Audrey's mother and Estelle's father were sister and brother

The creek had been their favorite meeting place for many years. It served as a bathing place, a swimming hole, and an all-around get away place. In the summer Audrey and Estelle swam, and in the fall they took long walks around the edge of the water, talking and catching up on family gossip. They shared their dreams of a future full of family, fun, and friends. During the winter, they made small fires in the shelters created by the large boulders surrounding the creek, using the fire for warmth and to parch peanuts in an old popcorn popper. Mostly the two met just to see each other and to share their feelings.

Audrey and Estelle really had not planned on going swimming. They were just escaping from the drudgery of their chores for a little while. Eventually the water looked too inviting, so in spite of all the rules—mostly old wives' tales they had grown up with—they could not resist a quick dip.

Looking at each other with identical smiles, the clothes began to fly in all directions until they were standing in their slips. Audrey bent over and reached between her legs, pulling the back of her slip to the front and securing it at her waist with a safety pin. Estelle followed Audrey's example, and within minutes they were splashing like five-year-olds.

"You don't go swimming after Labor Day," Audrey said in a singsong voice, "because you will get pneumonia."

"Yeah, and you don't get in the water if you are on your period, not even up to your ankles," added Estelle.

"Right, and you never wash your hair if it's that time of the month." Audrey gave Estelle a push causing her to sit down in the water with enough force to wet them both.

Laughing at each other, they splashed and giggled for long minutes, every so often grunting as they stepped on a sharp rock on the creek bed.

"We have to get out of here and dry off," Audrey said as she looked above the trees and saw the sun getting lower in the sky. "I have to get supper started." She gave Estelle another playful shove and ran up the bank.

"But we just got here." Estelle climbed up the bank. "Don't go yet." She shook her head back and forth slinging water everywhere.

"Watch it! You're getting me all wet."

"Very funny." Getting a little closer, Estelle shook her bouncy, red curls one more time. "Come on, I'll stop. Can't you stay a few more minutes? We haven't had a chance to talk about Billy Bartlett."

"The most mysterious boy in school." Audrey grabbed the blouse she had earlier tossed in the bushes and pulled it over her head as she let her slip drop to the ground.

"And the best looking."

"Okay, spill the beans! What do you know? Have you heard something new?" Hopping from one foot to the other, Audrey managed to step into her skirt, smiling at the sight of Estelle trying to get out of her wet slip.

"I found out that he and his mother came from Nashville."

"So? That still doesn't tell us a thing about them."

"No."

Laughing at Estelle and her attempts to get her hair dry by swinging it back and forth, Audrey climbed up on a rock, sat down, and started swinging her legs back and forth. She motioned for Estelle to sit beside her.

Billy and his mother had lived here a year, and because they kept to themselves and didn't join in the church outings they were the subject of gossip.

"Wonder why they moved to Double Springs, Alabama of all places?" Estelle plopped down on the boulder beside Audrey. "They don't have any family here."

"Wonder where Mr. Bartlett is?"

"Maybe there is no Mr. Bartlett. Maybe Mrs. Bartlett is really a Miss—"

"Estelle! What a nasty thing to say!"

"Well, what if she is a fallen woman?"

Audrey stared at the clear creek below. Breathing in the pine-scented air, she shivered. She crossed her arms over her chest holding her elbows. Was it a ghostly chill like her Grandma Nettie talked about—somebody was walking on your grave—or was it just Estelle's woeful words?

"A woman with a past."

"Please don't say that, it just seems too awful, I can't imagine not having a daddy. Maybe, he really did have a father and he died with a heart attack or something." Not having a complete family was the worst thing she could imagine. She didn't know if she felt more sorry for Billy or his mother.

"Maybe. Maybe not."

"Come on, I've really got to go home. Let's come back tomorrow. I'm going to be really nice to Billy Bartlett, just in case he is what you almost said."

"Me too!"

Giving Estelle a quick hug, Audrey bent over and picked up her wet slip and was already planning dinner as she waved goodbye.

You can see through a window to the outside world,
or that same window can reflect your own image.
A window can close you in or open up your world,
and when you have no windows,
you have your mind,
which can be more open than any window or door.

—Audrey Dickinson

CHAPTER ONE

1929

Audrey came awake with a start. Her heart was throbbing. What had startled her? A dream? No, she didn't think so, though she was feeling sluggish, sort of clammy.

Becoming aware of her surroundings, she began to get her bearings. She was in her own bed, in the small room her father Wesley Dickinson had built off the kitchen—the room she shared with Violet, her younger half-sister.

From the front of the house, she could hear him and his friends. They were still at it, cards and shine. Lord, how she hated whiskey. It made men and women so different.

Her father had never been mean or violent with her, but he became louder when he was drinking and lost all sense of what needed to be done. Or so it seemed. She could not find a good reason for him to make the stuff. Moonshine was what others called it. To Audrey, it was a sin to make the stuff, and she hated the smell as much as she hated the end result it caused.

As long as I'm awake, I may as well go down to the outhouse. She could use the porcelain pot under the bed, but she knew who would have to empty and clean it in the morning. That chore seemed worse than going out during the night, and she hated going out during the night. It wasn't so much that she was scared of the long walk in the dark. It was knowing her father's friends were still around, and they frightened her; and now that her beloved brother Purvey wasn't home, it seemed worse. She thought about waking Violet up to go with her, but she was so grumpy when she didn't get her sleep it hardly seemed worth the effort.

Stretching like a cat, she felt the texture of the cotton gown she had fashioned out of fertilizer sacks. It was rough and made her skin itch, but she knew that with several more washings it would become soft and pliable. With her mind still wandering, she slipped out of bed. She didn't want to wake Missy Violet at all costs. She walked through the kitchen, opened the door, and quietly stepped out on the back porch.

She knew the revelers were in the front of the house around the potbelly stove. Although it wasn't cold, they seemed to think that was the place to enjoy their cards and her father's own brand of moonshine.

As she made her way down the porch steps, she felt sure that her father and his friends didn't even know she and Violet were in the house.

* * * * *

When Thadius Eugene (Gene) Godwin lost the last hand of cards, he decided to see if he could find another one of Wesley's fruit jars—the ones filled with moonshine. Not that Wesley wasn't generous about passing the bottle around. Gene just had a need for a bigger sample. He wandered into the kitchen, being as quiet as a big man could be. He edged over to the door, bumped into the table, and righted a glass before it turned over. He leaned against the door to steady himself and peered out. He saw Audrey walking down the path, probably going to the toilet.

He had been noticing Audrey a lot of late. She was a slim little ol' gal, mite too slim for his liking. But those were firm looking breasts that he had been seeing beneath her cotton dresses. Wesley better watch that one.

Gene had a wife, a very nice wife, who was unfortunately very much pregnant at the moment. He had gotten down-right horny of late, as he was prone to tell anyone who would listen, because Gladys June didn't want nothin' to do with him, he would lament.

"I don't want nobody 'a rootin' around on me." she had told him recently.

Pushing himself away from the wall Gene opened the door and staggered out on the porch. "Damn, what's a feller supposed to do anyhow?"

Maybe Audrey's a meetin' somebody out there. Maybe for ol' Wesley's sake I just orta' go on out and see what that little filly is up to. She damn sure is a purty enough sight, a-walking in the moonlight.

"I might just orta' go on out here and relieve myself, while I'm a-doing Wesley this favor," he said aloud, not only to hear himself speak, but just in case someone had noticed him leaving the house.

Stumbling down the porch steps, he never took his eyes off the path to the outhouse. He stepped into the bushes, positioning himself so he could keep an eye on the direction Audrey had taken. From where he was standing, he could see her as she entered the toilet.

Just as he was getting ready to button up his fly, he heard the toilet door open and close. He took one more quick look back toward the house, then turned to watch her as she came up the walkway.

Maybe I'll just hold on to ol' Pete' a mite longer. Don't feel bad 't-all. Ol' Pete' you are a throbbing with a need for a woman. Damn Gladys; a man ort not have to play with hisself no how. It's all your fault Gladys June. You and your high minded ideas of what's right and wrong.

* * * * * *

Audrey dawdled as she walked back to the house. The stars were so bright, and it smelled like rain. Judging from the location of the moon, she knew it had to be close to midnight. She was already thinking about tomorrow. Her brother Purvey was coming home for a visit. The Sheriff had arranged for him to come for the weekend.

She was planning to fix them some roasted peanuts. She loved peanuts—roasted, boiled, or raw. It didn't make any difference to her, but Purvey liked them roasted best. Purvey was not only her brother. He was her best friend. In her eyes, the very worst thing that had ever happened to her was Purvey being away from home. It was awful with him gone.

"It won't be too much longer before he'll be home for good," the Sheriff had said recently.

She could hardly wait. If she only knew when, then she would have a day to look forward to. The not knowing for sure was what bothered her.

As she reached the first porch step, she felt someone grab her from behind, one hand over her mouth, the other on her left breast. She was so terrified she didn't fight at first. Then she was screaming in her head, for no noise was coming from her mouth.

3

She twisted and turned and kicked, trying to see who her attacker was. She was like a rag doll in his arms. As he pulled her around to the side of the house, her feet never touched the ground. Never once did his hand leave her mouth as he climbed into a wagon, dragging her with him.

The sound of her gown ripping was a roar in her ears. He was on top of her. Gasping for breath, she tried to move, tried harder to fight him off. Her hands were beating him on his head, his arms, wherever they landed she scratched as hard as she could.

She forced herself to open her eyes to see who was doing this to her. Gene Godwin, it was Eugene Godwin! What? Why? Why was he doing this to her?

Silently she was crying, the tears falling down her face. Scared and shaking, the fight was almost gone out of her.

He removed his hand from her mouth and covered it with his own. She could taste the foul smell of him. The liquor caused the bile to rise in her throat.

Oh, dear God, I'm going to throw up. What is Gene doing to me? Her gown was no longer covering her. She could feel his rough hands on her bare skin.

* * * * * *

Gene was past stopping, or going back to fondling himself. This was what he wanted—a real woman, one with a little fight in her. Gladys June had long since become so passive he didn't have no fun with her, even before she got pregnant.

Penetrating her soft body was another thing though. She was so stiff, and he was having a hard time getting her to keep her legs open.

Damn those little fists were getting to be a mite irritating, and with each blow he got a little rougher with her. He jerked her arms above her head using both of his hands to hold her down. He tried to kiss her on the mouth, but she kept twisting her head from side to side.

"Daddy. God. Help me. Please somebody help me!"

"Shut up!"

"Come on Gladys June, you know you like it when your man's a little rough." It was no longer Audrey beneath him, but his wife. He was reliving another time. He pushed harder, ramming himself into the soft body. He didn't notice she had stopped fighting. He didn't see the blood flowing down her legs. He was only aware of his own body and the release he wanted. At last spasms of pleasure overcame him.

"Oh, there. There. That's it!"

With his body finally satisfied he rolled off Audrey and hit the rough wagon with a loud thump, sleep came quickly.

By gosh an begorra,
I'll get to the bottom of this.
Somebody is going to pay.

—John Dickinson

CHAPTER TWO

"What was that?" Wesley Dickinson shoved his cane-back chair away from the table, causing cards to go flying and glasses full of moonshine to break on the hard, wood floor.

"Sounded like Gene," John Potter said as he followed Wesley out the front door. "Probably stepped in a briar patch, the drunken old fool."

Wesley could hear Fred Simpson stumbling around behind them. He never wanted to be left out of anything.

"I don't see him no wheres."

"That's the point, Fred, look for him." Wesley said as he stumbled off the steps. He even bent over and looked under the porch steps as if to prove his point.

It was Wesley who finally thought to look in the back of the wagon. He was the one who saw her first, bloody from the assault and lying so still, he thought she was dead! Wesley heard Gene snoring, and as his senses took in the whole sick mess, Wesley lost control. He grabbed Gene and pulled him out of the wagon.

Wesley was pounding on Gene. "You sorry piece of a man. What have you done to my little girl?"

Gene's beating was futile. Wesley, who never cried, was crying and shaking from head to foot. He wasn't making any sense of the beating or the reason for the beating.

John grabbed Wesley around the chest, pulling him away from Gene as he fell to the ground. Wesley had been holding him up trying to knock him down.

"Wesley, go take care of Audrey. We'll handle this," John said. "Right, Fred?"

Fred was bending over Gene. Wesley assumed he was trying to see if he was dead, but he took time to look up and nod his agreement to John.

"Just get the sheriff, before I kill him," Wesley yelled! His hoarse voice sounded as if it were coming from the depths of a hollow, empty well.

"Okay," Fred said, "I'll go get him. John, you stay here."

Wesley picked up Audrey's small, limp body. He tried to rearrange her torn bloodstained gown to cover her, the gown he had watched her make only days earlier. He carried her reverently into the house.

Tears flowing freely down his face he lay her in <u>his</u> bed. Even in the horror of the moment, he knew the bed she shared with Violet was not the place for her tonight.

He fell on his knees beside the bed, throwing his arm protectively over her, sobbing into the sheets.

"I'm so sorry, baby. I'm so sorry."

* * * * *

Sheriff Joe Bailey was used to being summoned to Wesley's house. The drunks sometimes got out of hand. But this took him by surprise.

Fred Simpson greeted him in the yard. "Sheriff, it looks like Gene had his way with Miss Audrey. She's pretty beat up."

John Potter walked up on the porch with him and pointed towards Wesley's bedroom. "In there."

Sheriff Bailey walked over to the bedroom door and glanced in. Taking a quick look at Audrey and seeing Wesley on the floor, he decided it was best to leave them alone for the moment.

He had never seen Wesley in such a state. He was surprised that Gene Godwin was still alive.

As he stepped back on the porch, he saw a neighbor lady walk into the yard. "Mary, please go see what you can do for Audrey. Let me know if we need to send for Doc Stanley."

Charles Peyton Stanley was the only doctor for miles around. Any and all medical problems were dumped on his doorstep. Sheriff Bailey figured this qualified as a medical problem.

"Sure will, Sheriff," Mary replied. "What's wrong with her? John didn't say when he fetched me. I just saw her this morning sweeping the yard, and she seemed to be fine. She's a mighty fine housekeeper."

"Mary if you will bear with me for a little bit I'll get it all straightened out. Wesley's with her now. If you don't mind, ask him to come out and see me a minute."

"Sure thing, Sheriff." Mary started to the back of the house, but the Sheriff reached over and touched her arm.

"She's in Wesley's room."

Going back out on the porch, Sheriff Bailey turned to John.

"You and Fred tell me what happened here." He looked at one then the other.

"Well, Sheriff, don't rightly know," Fred said. "We was all a-playing cards like we do sometimes, and was a tasting Wesley's home brew."

"Go on, Fred. We all know about Wesley and his home brew." Sheriff Bailey tried to get him to get on with his story. For it was a well-known fact in Winston County that Wesley Dickinson made his own brand of home brew. He, himself, had often sampled a few jars in his teenage years. Shaking his head as if to dislodge his present thoughts and get on with the situation at hand. He looked directly at Fred, waiting for an answer.

"Well, like I said, we was all a-playing cards when Gene there," Fred nodded towards Gene, who was stretched out in the yard, "left to get another drink or piss or something. Anywise, we kept on playing without him. We just figured he was mad 'cause John won the last hand."

"Don't know how long he was gone, Sheriff," John spoke up. "Like Fred said, we just kept on playing. Then we heard him scream out, like maybe he was hurt or something, so we all come on outside to look for him."

"Yeah, that's just the way it was, Sheriff."

"Well, go on, boys. Then what happened? What was Gene doing?" Sheriff Bailey prompted, getting a little impatient with the slowness of John and Fred's story.

John looked at Fred, and Fred looked at the ground, as if they were thinking that they didn't know how to tell the rest.

"Well?"

"She, Audrey, was a-layin' in the back of Gene's wagon, passed out and still as death. Wesley got to them first and pulled Gene from the wagon. Course there weren't no fight in Gene, Sheriff. He was all done in."

"Sheriff, it looked like Gene done had his way with the little gal. She was all bloody, and sure looked like she put up a fight. Gene was pretty scratched up on his face, and her gown was all torn up, and. . .

Well, Sheriff, I don't like to say it about nobody, but it sure looked like he had killed her. I'm sure that's what Wesley thought, the way he was beating on ol' Gene there."

"Then Wesley took Audrey in the house, and I came for you. And John went after Miss Mary. And that's all we know."

"I have been the sheriff in Winston County for twelve years, and I've never seen a situation like this."

He knew the Dickinsons. He helped get Wesley's boy, Purvey, out of town when he accidentally shot his stepmother. And he knew the Potters and the Simpsons. He helped Fred Simpson persuade that rambunctious Smith boy to make an honest woman out of Fred's oldest girl awhile back. He knew the Godwins real well. This wasn't Gene Godwin's style. Gene had a wife. Why, if he wasn't mistaken, she was as ripe as a watermelon right now, ready to bring their first young'un into the world.

He knew all these folks well. He'd gone to school with most of them. Poor Gladys. Poor Audrey. As all these thoughts passed through his mind, he decided the best thing to do was wait and see how Wesley wanted to handle the whole mess.

"Boys, help me get Gene in his wagon. Fred, drive him on home and have Gladys stick him in bed to sleep it off." The three of them lifted Gene off the ground and put him in the front of the wagon where he slumped over on the seat. Sheriff Bailey didn't have the stomach to put him in the back of the wagon, even though there wasn't anything out of place back there, and he sensed that Fred and John felt the same way.

As they propped him up, John reached over and closed Gene's gaping fly. "Miss Gladys don't need no reason to wonder what happened tonight."

"We'll just tell her for now that he fell in a briar patch," Fred spoke up. "That should explain some of the scratches."

"Boys," the Sheriff said, "let's keep this between us and let the dust settle on this little incident until we see how Wesley wants to handle it."

Fred and John nodded.

"It could have been one of our girls," Fred said quietly.

"What was Gene thinking about anyway?" John spouted. "Forcing that little ol' gal like that. I don't even want to think about it."

"I hope Wesley don't get carried away over this," Fred said, "I don't like it either, and Miss Audrey deserves better. But damn, Sheriff, it ain't gonna go down easy around here if it gets out."

"Go on now, boys, and get him on home, I'll finish up here." He waved the wagon on out of the yard. "Guess I better go see how Audrey is. Wesley too. They've been on the receiving end of enough tragedy in my book. They certainly don't need anymore."

He walked toward the house. Wasn't Purvey coming home tomorrow? Yep, he had personally arranged it. But maybe he should un-arrange it. He would have to ask Wesley. One more to add to his long list of questions for Wesley.

He opened the bedroom door and noticed that Audrey seemed to be sleeping. Wesley was sitting in a chair beside the bed, and Mary was standing at the washstand rinsing out what he assumed was Audrey's gown. He motioned for her to join him in the other room.

"Miss Mary, how is she?" He shut the bedroom door behind them.

"She's fine, Sheriff. I gave her something to sleep. It was pretty rough on her. She's torn, but she will heal."

"And Wesley?"

"He hasn't left her side, except when I chased him out to make her decent."

"Did she talk to you about it?"

"No, I didn't press her. She's been like a rag doll, letting me clean her up, not helping any."

"If you can stay, I'm gonna' let this wait till in the morning."

"I'll stay, Sheriff. Just stop on your way past my place and tell my man Orly, so's he won't worry none."

"I'll do that, Mary. Please tell Wesley I'll see him in the morning."

Mary nodded as she walked him to the door.

He stepped off the porch and looked up to the sky as if he might receive some unknown guidance. Sticking his hands in his pockets he walked quickly to his car. "Maybe tomorrow we can all see this a little differently. At least I hope so."

If God closes one door,
he will open another,
and if there are no doors
He'll open a window.

–Abraham Dickinson

CHAPTER THREE

Late in the afternoon the next day, Audrey still lay in the bed. She knew in her heart she needed to get up and do something, but it was so much easier to let the world go on around her, to stay where she was and think and think, to remember how things used to be. In remembering, she did not know how much she truly remembered and how much she only thought she remembered, for in the telling by others, she had adopted it all as her remembrance.

She remembered Grandpa John explaining all their family to her, how he and Grandma Nettie had so many children that he lost count. Grandma Nettie would always shake her head over his nonsense.

"Of course you remember them all," she would say. "He better, cause against my better judgement, he named each and every one of them."

Audrey smiled, thinking about Grandma Nettie. Her family was the only bright spot in her life right now.

There was her father Wesley and his three brothers, Monroe, Abraham, and McKinley. They were known most of their lives as John Dickinson's boys. There were also four sisters, Palestine, Margaret, Lisabeth, and Minnie May. Audrey's favorite was her Uncle Monroe, for he loved music and good times. Uncle Monroe did not have a serious bone in his body, and because of this, all the young people loved him.

Her grandfather was a red-haired Irishman, full of humor and bad temper. Grandpa John had a phrase or saying for most everything, and in the Dickinson family his word was law. Little went on that he didn't know about or express an opinion about.

"By gosh and begorra I'll get to the end of whatever's going on," he would say, and there wasn't a person in Winston County who doubted his word on that.

Audrey wished with all her heart Grandpa John was here now. Maybe he could make sense of what happened to her.

Why do I feel so guilty and ashamed? What did I do? What have I ever done to deserve this? Why is God punishing me like this? I don't understand.

She could not rest for thinking. At first, she relived the attack. Then it was easier to think about her family rather than herself.

Maybe Uncle Abraham would know what do. Grandma always said he was just like Abraham in the Bible, a God-fearing man. Maybe Uncle Abraham could tell her why. Preachers were supposed to understand why this stuff happened. Right, God? Uncle Abraham was a preacher, a hell-fire and brimstone Baptist preacher, and Grandma Nettie's pride and joy.

Uncle Monroe could play music for her, but he wouldn't help her much with God.

"Poor daddy," she whispered, turning on her side to face the wall. "He's probably beside himself. First Purvey and now this. Grandma Nettie was always a-worrying over Daddy. He looks the most like Grandpa, but Daddy and God just never found their footing."

Her father did not have Uncle Abraham's love of God or the need to walk the straight and narrow way, according to Grandma Nettie. If it were not for that Dickinson look, as Grandma Nettie called it, she would not have believed he belonged to her. Daddy was a bother to her, mostly because of his wild ways and chosen profession.

"Poor Grandma," she said, drawing her knees up to her chest. She wrapped her arms around herself, holding tightly. "Daddy is a bootlegger and most everyone knows it."

He liked to call it "home brew." It was really whiskey in a fruit jar. Grandma Nettie prayed for him all the time, but he didn't change any before she died.

She remembered Grandma Nettie telling Uncle Abraham, "I'm a-puttin' Wesley in your hands, and I'm expecting you and God to work it out."

Grandma Nettie died knowing in her heart that her boy was going to see the error of his ways. "When?" Had always been the question she asked.

Audrey turned on to her back and rubbed her left shoulder. It felt so stiff and sore. She knew she was bruised in other places. She had heard Mary gasp when she was cleaning her up. Mary had been so kind. One day, she would tell her so.

She was aware of her surroundings. Getting up was another story. She did not have the energy or fortitude or whatever it took to make herself move.

Closing her eyes, she pretended to be asleep. Her Daddy had been checking on her off and on all day, and he was at the door again. She could feel his presence even if she didn't smell the cigarette she knew he was holding. It seemed to comfort him when he found her asleep.

She would not disappoint him.

You can have all the
babies you want.
All I need is Wesley.

—Selah Miller Dickinson

CHAPTER FOUR

Selah Miller married Wesley Dickinson when she was about twenty. Most folks said she got the worst of it, but Selah didn't think so. She felt she had waited a long time for marriage, longer than most of her friends who were married at thirteen and fourteen. Even Abraham, Wesley's brother, had married Viola when she was only thirteen.

Selah thought a lot about Abraham and Viola, sorta' wondering how life with a preacher was. Well, one thing that was certain, life was never dull with Wesley. He knew how to court a girl. In Selah's eyes, he was special.

She and Viola were great friends and Selah loved to go to their house. Viola and Abraham were well on their way to having a house full of babies. They already had two boys, and Viola looked a little family-minded again. Although she loved Viola and her babies, Selah would be okay if the babies never came to her house. She and Wesley had each other and that was enough for Selah.

Selah's mother died when Selah was eighteen months old. None of the Miller women lived past thirty-five. Selah didn't know why exactly, but she planned on being different. Maybe having babies made you go sooner. If so, she certainly didn't want any.

Wesley had a regular job at the sawmill, but on the side he had a still and made moonshine. Selah knew. She even washed fruit jars for him, but she let on to Nettie, and especially to Abraham, that she didn't know what Wesley was up to. Wesley would put the pure moonshine in fruit jars, then bury them up in the woods to let them age a bit before he sold them.

Selah, who was an excellent seamstress, made him a long, dark coat with many pockets, all on the inside. He would carry fruit jars with his latest batch in the pockets, clanging as he walked. Wesley was always cold, thin blood he claimed, so the coat served two purposes: a walking store and a garment for warmth.

Selah had one brother, Joe. He and his wife, Dolly, were frequent visitors. They were visiting the day Selah was so sick she could barely get out of bed. "Sealey," Dolly questioned, "you been regular lately?"

"What on earth do you mean Dolly?" Selah asked as she became dizzy and sat back down on the bed she had just left.

"Well Sealey, you look and act like Miz Barker did when she were a-carryin' them twin boys."

"Oh my God, Dolly, you could be right! A baby, me? Good Lord, I hope not."

Dolly was correct, and seven months later Purvey was born. Selah and Wesley waited almost five more years before she again became pregnant, and this time it was a girl. Audrey Annell Dickinson was born in the fall of 1911, looking like a true Irish Dickinson with baby blue eyes, blonde hair, and an English complexion of peaches and cream, a real beauty.

She was Wesley's pride and joy, and on the day of her birth Wesley walked three miles to tell his parents, Nettie and John, that their new granddaughter had arrived.

Of course, his part in the birth had been quite limited as he was out delivering his latest batch of brew when Audrey decided it was time to enter this world. But in the telling of her beauty, his part became larger and larger until Nettie remarked; "I'm beginning to think he carried that child for nine months instead of Selah."

Selah had a hard time in birthing Audrey, and she never regained her health. The Dickinson women pitched in and helped with Audrey, so she became the community child—much loved and much cared for.

Selah died when Audrey was three.

Peanuts are good for your soul.

I'm pretty sure that's in the Bible.

If not, I know I heard it in church.

—Purvey Dickinson

CHAPTER FIVE

Purvey's life changed very little when Selah died. He still had his precious little sister Audrey and his father, Wesley. They both doted on Audrey, making sure she did not want for anything. There were plenty of aunts, uncles, and cousins, so she never seemed to miss their mother but only knew there was one less person to do her bidding.

Purvey was about fifteen when Wesley married again, this time to Renee Baker, who was already expecting at the time. She also brought to the marriage two children from her previous marriage, Sally Jo and Betty Sue, who stayed mostly with their father's family.

Violet was born about five months after the marriage. For whatever reason, Purvey never felt like Violet was really his sister. He did not have the same feelings for her as he did Audrey, and Audrey seemed to feel the same way. Perhaps their opinion was shaped from living with the Dickinson women. Palestine and Viola did not approve of this marriage and readily said so out of Wesley's hearing.

"Purvey, do you think Violet looks anything like me or you?" Audrey asked as she brushed Violet's hair.

"Not particularly, but remember that old dog of Grandpa John's that had all them funny looking pups? They didn't look much like their mother either."

Purvey was always making comparisons. He had his doubts about Violet's parentage, but he didn't see any harm in Audrey not knowing that. Violet did not resemble the Dickinson family but was more like her mother, Renee.

Audrey was always trying to make Violet look clean, which seemed to be a full time job. She was a very overweight child and her mother Renee didn't care much about cleanliness, so how Violet or the other girls looked was never an issue with her in their home.

Audrey, having spent all her early years with the Dickinson women, set great store in being clean, which included her surroundings as well as her personal self. Purvey was on the receiving end of a lot of Audrey's ideas for cleaning up. Purvey wondered if Audrey even knew the difference between men's work and women's work, since she was always wanting him to scrub something.

Purvey and Audrey were very close. They stuck up for each other, and Renee and her children got the worst of it, when Wesley wasn't around.

When Purvey was about sixteen, Wesley went up to Haleyville in hopes of buying a new mule. He left home early that morning with plans on being home by nightfall. As dusk settled in, Renee got tired of holding supper for Wesley's return. It was starting to get a little cooler, getting darker earlier and earlier. Renee was ready to get the children in the house and the house closed up for the night.

"Audrey, get that table set, and take the beans and cornbread up, they're done enough." She motioned towards the table over in the corner. Audrey was going on twelve, and Renee loved to order her around. Basically she was a good girl, but she hadn't wanted her daddy to marry Renee. Sometimes those feelings came to the surface, and Audrey had a hard time being an obedient child.

It wasn't a happy household with Purvey and Audrey always sticking up for each other and ignoring the other children.

They thought they were too good for them was Renee's opinion. Well she would show them. This was her home, and she was in charge.

"Where is Wesley anyhow? He was supposed to be home long before this." Renee knew she was talking to herself, but she didn't care. "Probably off somewhere drunk!" Still talking to herself, Renee sat down at the table to have her supper.

Wesley usually did most of his drinking at home since he liked his home brew better than anyone else's, but, knowing him, he probably took some to bargain with on the mule and then drank his way through the buying. Regardless, he was late, and Renee wasn't too happy about it.

"Renee, where do you think Daddy is?" Purvey asked as he reached for the bowl of potatoes.

"How should I know? He never tells me nothing! Ya'll eat your supper, and get this mess cleaned up." Renee didn't do much in the way of cleaning up. She left that to Sally, her daughter by her first marriage, and Audrey, mostly Audrey. Sally, like her mother, didn't care much for housekeeping. They did not see the necessity of making beds and doing dishes too often.

Purvey was getting a little anxious about his father being gone. He felt responsible for all the women in his life. They had just finished supper when they heard a noise outside. Purvey jumped up and got the gun. "Stay here and I'll see who it is!"

"No, Purvey! Get away from there! It might be Wesley." Renee pushed herself up from the table and knocked her chair over in her hurry to get to Purvey.

Purvey was striding across the room with the gun up and ready by the time Renee was on her feet. Renee ran after him and tried to take the gun away.

Audrey was walking across the kitchen floor on her way to the sink, with her hands full of dirty dishes, when the gun went off. It sounded like a cannon in that small house.

It all happened so fast, yet it was like time had stopped—Purvey going toward the door and Renee behind him grabbing for the gun.

"Oh my God!" Audrey screamed. "Oh my God, Purvey, you shot Renee!"

Indeed he had. Renee looked at him with a startled look, an unbelieving stare. She didn't say a word. She just looked from Audrey to Purvey and back again. She was sitting upright on the floor holding her upper thigh and then, as if it were just the most normal thing, lay back on the rug and closed her eyes.

For the rest of his life, Purvey knew he would remember that look.

Dropping the dishes, Audrey ran to Renee, grabbing a towel as she went. Falling on her knees beside Renee, she tried to see how bad it was. Purvey was on his knees on the opposite side of Renee, having dropped the gun. He had one hand over his mouth and the other wiping the tears he was trying not to cry.

Audrey reached over and shook Purvey to get his attention. "Go, Purvey! Go get some help! Now! Right now, Purvey, go! Renee is hurt bad; go get Miss Elliot! She's the closest!"

"Purvey, are you listening to me?" Since the gun shot, the house was painfully quiet. Sally was standing in the doorway to the back of the house as if she didn't know which direction she should go. Purvey still hadn't moved from his position. Thank God Violet was staying at her grandmother's house, where she had been for the past couple of days.

Wesley's children are spoiled rotten brats.
He never thinks they do nothin'
wrong, but I'm here to tell you
they are just plain spoiled.

—Renee Dickinson

CHAPTER SIX

Hundreds of thoughts ran through Audrey's mind as she tried to take charge of the situation. Renee had been shot in the upper thigh. The gun was so close to her when it went off it looked like her leg was burned. Her leg was black-looking and blood was everywhere.

Purvey was shaking all over, and he didn't seem to comprehend what Audrey was saying to him. He watched her lips as she spoke, but didn't respond.

Audrey jumped up, yelling at Sally and Purvey at the same time. "Sally, get some water and a rag. Purvey, get going, or I'm gonna' get that gun after you!"

Finally Purvey jumped up and ran to the door. He looked back once at Audrey and Sally saying, "I didn't mean to, I didn't mean to, Audrey, Sally. You believe me don't you?"

"I know, Purvey. It was an accident; now go get Miss Elliot."

Audrey began sponging Renee's forehead with the cool water that Sally had brought her. She had Sally sit down, and placed her mother's head in her lap. Audrey gave Sally the wet rag and had her take over wiping Renee's face while she got more towels. It was an endless job trying to keep the blood wiped up. All the while Audrey was talking to Renee and Sally, praying and talking; and after awhile she didn't know if she were praying or talking, or if it was just one long, drawn out prayer.

"Where is that Purvey? Why isn't he back yet?" Nobody answered that question. Renee just kept bleeding. Audrey didn't know what else to do except to sit there wiping up the blood while she encouraged Sally to keep the cool rag on her mother's head.

As Miss Elliot, her two boys, and Purvey came through the door, Audrey looked up with doe eyes, full of tears. Looking from Miss Elliot to Renee, she didn't seem to realize she and Sally had as much blood on them as Renee had on her.

"Thank God, you're here, Miss Elliot. Renee has been shot. She is so still. I'm so glad you are here."

"It's gonna' be okay, Audrey honey," Miss Elliot said. "Boys, get her on the bed. My man Ezra has gone to fetch the doctor. Where's Wesley?"

"We don't know, he was supposed to be home by now. He went to Haleyville to buy a mule and to get some supplies." Now that Miss Elliot was here, Audrey was wringing her hands and talking so fast her words were tumbling out one on top of the other.

* * * * *

It was close to two hours later when Wesley came through the door, dirty from head to foot. He had bought the mule and had tried to ride him to his dismay, for he had promptly been thrown into a mud puddle. It had been a long journey home with that stubborn mule.

He was not expecting anything when he came through the door except a hot meal, and someone to listen to his tall tales all about his harrowing day with that damned ol' mule that might be mule meat tomorrow if he didn't mend his ways.

Everyone was talking at once trying to tell him what happened as Doctor Stanley walked in with Ezra Elliot.

"Where's she at?" Doctor Stanley asked no one in particular.

"She's in the other room. I had the boys put her in the bed. She has lost a lot of blood. We did what we could," Miss Elliot tried to explain as the doctor walked in the direction she had pointed.

"Wesley, you better sit down and let these young'uns' tell you what happened here tonight," Ezra pulled out a chair at the table for Wesley and motioned for Purvey to get him a drink of water.

Sally had followed Doctor Stanley and Miss Elliot back to the bedroom where her mother was, so it looked like the tellin' was going to be up to Audrey. Purvey still looked like he might pass out any minute; so Audrey, squaring her shoulders, began to tell Wesley and her other listeners what happened.

"We heard a noise outside and Purvey wanted to go see what it was. He took the gun down off the mantle and started towards the door with the gun up, like he was ready to shoot someone. Renee jumped up to stop him. She grabbed for the gun; and when she pulled Purvey's arm down, the gun went off. She's shot in the leg!" The words spilled out one on top of each other, and little did Audrey know how many times she would have to repeat that story. Over and over again as each relative and neighbor asked, the story was again repeated.

Doctor Stanley walked back into the kitchen and asked to see Wesley outside. They all fell silent as Wesley and the doctor walked out the back door.

"Wesley, she has lost a lot of blood. Right now she is in a coma and doesn't seem to be in any pain. I've done all I can do for her. I'll stay till it's over, however long that takes. I don't think she will make it through the night."

Wesley dropped down on the steps of the back porch and sat there. No words came to his brain or his mouth. What could he possibly say?

"In the morning we will have to get the sheriff. Something like this has to be reported. For now, Wesley, you might want to prepare the children for the worst and send someone for Renee's people."

Renee did not regain consciousness before she died, she just slipped quietly away as her family hovered over her whispering to each other about her and her life.

The sheriff stayed away until after the funeral, which was a very simple affair. Wesley buried Renee in the church cemetery. Mount Carmel Church was down the road, and it seemed like the right thing to do. For two Sundays after her death, Wesley and the children showed up for services. In spite of some of the whispered comments, the roof did not cave in from the sight of Wesley Dickinson in church.

* * * * *

Sheriff Bailey questioned Audrey and Sally and compared their story with Purvey's. He then spoke to the doctor about Renee's injuries.

"Sheriff, looks to me like the children are telling the truth. The powder burns were caused by the closeness of the gun when it fired, which is just like Audrey said, the gun was right against her when it went off.

Knowing what he did about the Dickinson household and the relationship between Wesley's children and Renee, Sheriff Bailey decided to take the matter up with Judge Parker. He felt that Judge Bennett was too close to Renee's family, and it might influence his judgment on this one.

Judge Parker talked with him on two different occasions before deciding a trial would not be warranted. They decided, considering Purvey's age, that it would serve no purpose other than to make him bitter if they sent him to jail, which might have been the outcome of a trial.

Renee's family refused to believe it was an accident and would most likely try to see that he was tried for murder.

Sheriff Bailey found a boys' reform school up near Ridgeville, Alabama, not so far away that Purvey couldn't come home for visits if his behavior were in keeping with their rules. It was a suitable place, one that would satisfy a judge.

Judge Parker called Wesley and Purvey into his office and told them his ruling on the case.

"Wesley, I'm going to send Purvey to a reform school for a minimum of four years. I realize Purvey will soon be considered a man, but there are others there his age who are training for jobs." Judge Parker continued speaking as he signed the papers to seal his orders.

Looking over his glasses he said, "Purvey, you will be with a group of young men your age. I think it's best if you leave Double Springs for awhile. Hopefully, by the time you return, the community's feelings about the shooting will be a thing of the past."

The entire town knew that Purvey and his stepmother did not see eye-to-eye on any subject. Far too many people did not think it was an accident.

There was no trial, only the judge and the sheriff putting their heads together deciding Purvey's future.

* * * *

That seemed like the beginning of the end to Audrey. Not only did she lose her brother and best friend, her protector from Wesley's rowdy friends, but also Renee, who in spite of everything, was a mother of sorts to her. Now Audrey had to fill two roles: mother to Violet and housekeeper for Wesley. The other Baker children went to live with their father's family.

The day Purvey left, he and Audrey vowed to write often and never to give up hope.

It was remembering Purvey and all that had happened to him since Renee's death that pulled Audrey out of her stupor. "Purvey is coming home," Audrey spoke out loud. They were the first words she had spoken since Wesley had found her in the back of Gene's wagon.

"Daddy, what day is this? Purvey is supposed to come home!" Audrey's yell made Wesley jump up from the table where he had been sitting. He had to admit he was dozing. Damned it was good to hear that girl's voice. By gosh and begorra, it sounded like his little girl was back to herself.

"Sure is, honey, surely is." Wesley said, his mouth curving into his first smile in days, as he stood up and walked to Audrey's room. This he wanted to see for himself, his little girl back to herself, making plans for Purvey's homecoming.

The law says you are innocent
until proven guilty.
In this case there doesn't
seem to be much doubt.

—Sheriff Joe Bailey

CHAPTER SEVEN

Sheriff Joe Bailey made a point to keep his word whenever possible. He considered eight o'clock as early as most folks would want to see him. True to his word, he drove into Wesley's yard at 8:05.

He had already notified the authorities at Ridgeville that next weekend would be a better time to let Purvey Dickinson come home for his scheduled visit. "I certainly hope Wesley will agree with that decision," Joe said as he got out of the car. Sometimes he thought the only way to get a handle on what was going on was to just up and say it out loud. He tried not to talk out loud around folks though, in case they didn't agree with his thinking. Being an elected official did have its drawbacks. You did have to appear sane.

Looking toward the house he saw Wesley sitting on the front porch having a cup of coffee, which he assumed Miss Mary had made for him. Hope he didn't hear me talking to myself. He made a mental note to try to look around to see who might be listening in the future before he started gabbing out loud.

"Mornin', Wesley. Got any more of that coffee?"

"Sure, Sheriff, sit on down there, and I'll get you a cup." Wesley gestured to an empty rocker and walked on into the house, coming back a few minutes later with a fresh cup for himself and one for the sheriff.

"How's Audrey this morning?"

"Fine".

Joe knew Wesley wasn't given to long speeches, but he figured he would be full of talk this morning. Guess not. Looked like he was going to have to drag it out of him.

"Wesley, I thought you and Audrey might rather wait till next weekend for Purvey to pay his visit, so I arranged it this morning. Hope that suits you." Joe spoke quickly, as he fished in his pocket for his Prince Albert can and papers. Taking his time, he rolled himself a smoke, looking over at Wesley as he took a long drag.

"Oh, was it this weekend he was a-comin'? I forgot. Audrey handles all that stuff. Guess she forgot to tell me, or maybe she was a-fixin' to tell me a-fore she was taken advantage of." Wesley looked up at the sheriff as he spoke. His voice sounded whispery, not at all like his usual loud banter, but Sheriff Bailey still heard and understood the anger that was behind the words.

"Wesley, sooner or later we are gonna' have to talk about what happened here last night. I sent Gene on home, but this isn't something you can keep quiet for long. I was just waiting to see how you wanted to handle it."

"Arrest the bastard! Throw him in jail! I want him punished for what he did to my little girl." The seething anger Wesley was feeling was apparent in his voice. With both arms in the air and one of them pointing directly at the sheriff, Wesley shouted, "The last time I heard, rape was a crime. Right, sheriff?"

"That's true, Wesley." Even though Joe agreed in theory, Wesley's answer took him by surprise, or maybe it really didn't. He had thought maybe because of the circumstances, Wesley might want to keep it quiet and, if not forget that it happened, at least save Audrey from any unnecessary publicity and gossip.

"Wesley, if I arrest him, there is going to be a scandal, and Audrey will suffer from it, not Gene Godwin." Joe tried to reason with Wesley, seemingly getting no where.

"He hurt her. She never did nothing to be hurt like that, and I want him to take his medicine."

"What if we talk to Gene and see if he won't make some sort of restitution here?"

Wesley looked at Joe like he had lost his mind. "Restitution? For what? For accidentally abusing my little girl? Not on your life, this was no accident. He attacked Audrey. He physically attacked her. Hell, he could have killed her!" Shaking his head in disbelief, Wesley stood up so fast the rocker he had been setting in continued to rock. He turned and started back in the house, dismissing Joe with a wave of his hand. "That's absurd!"

"Now, Wesley, I'm not a-saying Gene was right." He reached out to stop Wesley as he walked past his chair.

Wesley shook off his hand, continuing toward the door.

"He wasn't right, Wesley! I'm just a-trying to do the right thing by everyone here. Trying to look out for Audrey and Gladys June." In spite of himself he was impressed with Wesley. The man was trying to hang on, trying not to break down, no doubt for Audrey's sake. Why, in his place he would have probably shot Gene and thought about it later. No, that wasn't Wesley's style; he didn't take much to killin'. Wonder what Wesley's style really is?

"I want him in jail, he can stand trial for this like any other common, low down, good-for-nothing bastard would." Wesley was pacing back and forth across the small porch now, waving his arms up and down as he tried to express himself. "Sheriff? Joe? That's what I want. That is the way I want it handled. If you won't do your duty, I'll go to Haleyville and get the Sheriff there to do it!"

"Wesley, what does Audrey think about all this? Is that what she wants too?" The Sheriff asked the questions, figuring he already knew the answers. *Nobody was going to do what Audrey wanted, no matter what that was. This was men business!*

"Just do it, Joe, just arrest him, and that is all I'm gonna' say on the subject." Wesley walked into the house and slammed the door behind him.

"Wait, Wesley. Can I talk to Audrey about this?"

"Nope, she don't want to see nobody!" Wesley spoke loudly behind the closed door, not offering to continue the conversation or re-open the door.

Throwing his cigarette in the yard, Sheriff Bailey stood up. Well, that settled it. Wesley didn't seem to be open to any of his suggestions, not that he blamed him. *Guess my next stop better be Thadius Eugene Godwin's place.*

Wonder if he remembers what happened here and if he has told Gladys to expect me? I doubt it. I really doubt it.

The last time he saw Gene he didn't look like he could remember his own name.

They told me he fell in
a briar patch.
That could happen,
don't you think?

—Gladys June Godwin

CHAPTER EIGHT

When Joe got to Gene's house, Gladys June was hanging her laundry up on the clothesline on the side of the house. "Morning, Gladys, where's Gene."

"He's still in bed, Sheriff."

"Wake him up, I'll be back in an hour," he told Gladys. "We got a few things to talk about."

Leaving Gladys looking a little bewildered, Joe drove on over to Fred Simpson's place.

Taking into consideration Gene's condition the night before, he had decided he would take Fred or John with him when he arrested Gene. He still didn't think arresting him was going to do that much good. He knew Gene would be out on bail by late afternoon, with the Godwins being so well known and having more money than most. It was true he didn't really know how to handle the situation. He was just hoping there was a way to avoid the scandal. Knowing people, he figured something like this wouldn't stay quiet anyway. Things like this always got out.

It was a short drive from Gene's place to Fred and Joanne's. The families were close, often visiting back and forth. Fred and Joanne Simpson were on their front porch when he drove up, almost like they were expecting him.

"Mornin', Fred, Miss Joanne," Joe said, could I see Fred alone for a minute?" From the look on Joanne's face she knew why he wanted to see Fred. *Oh, well*, Joe shrugged, *so much for keeping things quiet.*

As soon as Joanne went in the house, Joe turned to Fred. "How 'bout going over to Eugene Godwin's with me? I've got to arrest him, and I'd like a little support." He shook his head from side to side. "Not that I think there will be a problem. I just think it might help if some-one who was there came with me."

"Sure, Sheriff, I'll go. Can't seem to settle down and get anything done around here anyway. We were talking about whether I should plow the lower twenty acres today. You know Joanne thinks a man orta' work seven days a week," Fred said while putting his cap on. "Now, myself, I think Saturday should be a day of rest, like Sunday!"

Joe knew Fred was a good man, he just wasn't cut out to be a farmer, but Joanne's folks had left her this place, and he was trying to do right by her.

"Joanne," Fred called out, "I'm gonna' mosey over to Gene Godwin's with the sheriff."

Joanne stuck her head out the front door in acknowledgment.

Sheriff Bailey figured she hadn't been far away from that door or the window during the whole conversation. Oh well, he was sure Fred would fill her in sooner or later.

The Sheriff owned one of the few cars in Winston County. The voters had agreed that if he was going to do a good job, he needed more than a horse and buggy. They had come a long way, or maybe just liked the idea of their sheriff having a car. True, it was used, but it did get him around in a hurry.

When they drove up Gene was sitting on the front porch with Gladys hovering over him. Not much conversation on the way over, it was as if he and Fred were both lost in their own thoughts, none of which were good.

"Mornin' again, Gladys June. Howdy, Gene. Can Fred and I have a word with you alone? It won't take long."

Gladys looked a little put out as she walked back in the house. She left without questioning either Fred or Joe, but she did look sideways at Gene, perhaps she knew or felt something wasn't quite right with all this.

"Gene, I have to take you in for last night. Do you want to tell Gladys goodbye, or put your shoes on, or do anything that needs doing before we go?" He had decided to just spit it out and not waste any more time.

Gene looked like he had been shot. "What on earth for, Sheriff? Since when is it a crime to get a little drunk and fall into a briar patch?"

Evidently Gladys June had passed on the story the boys had told her to cover the scratches on Gene's face.

This was going to be harder than Joe thought. Fred was no help. He was leaning against the porch post, resting his weight on first one foot then the other as he tried unsuccessfully to roll a smoke.

Gene was looking at Fred as if he could help him come to some conclusion. "What did I do, Sheriff?" he finally asked.

"Eugene Godwin, you are under arrest for the rape of Audrey Dickinson."

Gene turned white and slumped over, putting his face in his hands, his elbows resting on his knees. "I never, Sheriff. . . I never...did I?"

The question was so low Sheriff Bailey wasn't sure he had heard him say anything. "Let's go, Gene, and get this over with."

A seemingly broken man, Gene stood up. At first it looked like he was going to go inside in search of Gladys June, but he brushed it away like swatting a fly. He turned and walked out toward the car.

"Fred, tell Gladys where we're taking Gene." Joe said. He walked around Gene and opened the door for him.

Leaning against the car with his legs and arms crossed, Joe waited for Fred to go talk to Gladys. He could hear Fred mumbling to himself. He didn't seem to want the chore he had assigned to him.

"Damn the sheriff and Eugene Godwin too." Fred said. "What am I supposed to say to her, anyway?"

"What was that, Fred, did you say something?" Joe thought it sure sounded like Fred was cussing.

"Nothing, Joe, just trying to figure out what I want to say here." He turned and walked up on the porch and called out to Gladys. "Gladys June, you in there? Can you come outside a minute?"

Gladys June came out on the porch, wiping her hands on the apron that covered her extended abdomen. "Fred? Where's Gene?" She looked at him with a puzzled look on her face.

"I just wanted to tell you, me and the sheriff are gonna' take Gene down to the jail. There was a little problem last night over at the Dickinson place. You might want to get a-hold of Gene's daddy and have him meet us there." Fred turned and practically ran out to the car, before Gladys could ask any questions.

To the sheriff she looked shocked and unprepared for what she had just heard. She probably couldn't think of anything to say or ask.

Gene, Fred, and the sheriff drove the four or five miles to town in complete silence. You could have heard a pin drop had they been in a room somewhere. As it was, all you heard was the sound of the motor and plenty of wind noise with all four windows open. *Fresh air was what this situation needs*, or so Sheriff Bailey thought.

The street was fairly quiet outside the courthouse. He was glad. Just the usual crowd of hangers-on. Pretty much like any other Saturday morning. Quiet, only a few fellows swapping yarns while the women folk shopped. Their arrival made little impression on anyone. Someone could have wondered why Eugene Godwin was walking around barefoot down at the jail, but not a word was spoken or a look conveyed by anyone.

It didn't take the Sheriff long to have his deputy, Harry, get Gene booked and placed downstairs in the holding cell. Twenty minutes later, as he was making arrangements to send Fred home, old man Godwin showed up looking like he could chew nails and spit them out, and Sheriff Bailey just might be on his list of possible appetizers.

"Calm down, Ben, I'll be with you in a minute," he held up his hand in a stopping gesture.

Turning his back to Ben, he repeated his earlier instructions to Harry. "Take Fred home, then come back by Judge Bennett's place and tell him he is needed over here."

"Yes sir," Harry said. Taking a wide berth around Ben Godwin, Harry and Fred went out the door, both glad to leave the Sheriff to handle Ben alone.

"Okay, Ben, let's make this easy on ourselves. I'm gonna' let you go down and see Eugene. Maybe he can explain a few things to you while we wait on Judge Bennett. You know the procedure. The Judge will set bail, and then we can go from there."

"Not so fast, Bailey. Yes, I know the procedures, but I want to know what you think my boy's done? His wife didn't know shit!"

"Ben, I'd rather Eugene tell you, but if that's the way you want it."
"It is!"

"It seems Eugene forced himself on Wesley Dickinson's oldest girl last night, rape... Ben. She was in pretty bad shape when last I saw her."

"No, no! Eugene couldn't, ... wouldn't do that. Who says it was Eugene?" Ben was pacing back and forth in the small office, clasping and unclasping his hands. "Who, I'm asking you who? Who says it was my boy?"

"Fred Simpson, John Potter. They were both there. Wesley found them first. Gene was pretty drunk. Ben, I know that is no excuse, but I don't think he remembers much about it."

"Fred? John? They're both old friends. They wouldn't lie about something like that. What's Wesley gonna do?"

"Well right now, Ben, he's willing to put it in the hands of the law. I tried to get him to settle this quietly on the side, but no way! Wesley was quite adamant about that. He wants Gene punished for what he did, and, quite frankly, we should all be happy he is willing to let the law handle it. Ben you know as well as I do, if this was his old man, John Dickinson, he would have probably handled it himself and left me the pieces to pick up."

"No, sheriff, he's right. It's better this way. If it had been Linda Sue I'd have been sitting in jail. I would have killed him!"

"Isn't Linda Sue about Audrey's age?"

Ben nodded. "Just a few months difference."

Sheriff Bailey figured Ben had to feel the pain Wesley was feeling; just imagining it could have been one of his own. In other circumstances, who knows what Ben would have done.

"I'm glad we are dealing with Wesley here and not John Dickinson. That old man didn't have a lick of sense when it came to his children." Ben rubbed his neck, finally looking the sheriff in the eye. "Eugene is my only son. Sheriff, what do I do now? Help me."

"Well, Ben, Judge Bennett will hear the evidence and set bail. After that there will be a hearing, then a trial, if the prosecutor decides to push it. Frankly Ben I'm not sure. Rape is a new one on me!"

"Thanks, I'll see Eugene now. If you will let me?"

Ben Godwin, who had sailed into Sheriff Bailey's office ready for a fight a few minutes before, now looked like an old man who had lost his dearest possession and did not know where to look for it.

Judge Bennett wasn't too pleased being dragged into town on a Saturday morning, but once presented with the facts he quit complaining and set bail at $150.00. It wasn't that he didn't take the charges seriously, but he knew that Eugene Godwin wouldn't go anywhere, regardless of the amount of the bail. Old man Godwin was a hard man, but he was fair; and it would be his money taking care of this mess.

It took Ben until four-o'clock to get the money together. Gene Godwin was on the street by 4:30, his daddy and momma with him.

Ben told him "Gladys June decided to wait on you at home. Can't say that I blame her. I'd like to be home myself."

The Sheriff cautioned Gene to stay available, that he would be notified of the time and date of the hearing.

Having dispensed with Gene and Ben, the sheriff decided another trip to Wesley's was warranted.

* * * * *

Doctor Stanley was just leaving as Joe pulled in to Wesley's yard.

"Sheriff," Doctor Stanley acknowledged him.

"How is she, Doc?"

"She's gonna live, Sheriff. She's a strong girl—bruised and traumatized, but she'll make it. The whole thing's a shame, though. What got into Gene Godwin anyway?"

"Thanks, Doc. Can't rightly say."

"Right, didn't figure you could. I'll see you back in town."

Joe nodded as he watched the doctor start up his car and drive away. Turning around he spoke to Wesley, who seemed to be patiently waiting to see what he wanted. "Evening, Wesley."

"Well, did you do like I wanted? Did you arrest him?" Wesley's anger hadn't diminished any. His sober look didn't do much to hide the anger that his clenched fists were portraying.

"Yes, Wesley, I arrested him. Ben got him out on bail about an hour ago."

"That figures." Wesley nodded. "He didn't try to deny it? Did he?"

"No, Wesley, he didn't, although, I don't really think he remembers."

No life is perfect, I guess.
Just look around, somebody
always has it a little
worse than you do.

—Granny Hunter

CHAPTER NINE

Nobody asked Audrey what she felt or what she wanted. It was such an embarrassing situation to them all, that few people, least of all those closest to her, would think of bringing up the subject. With nobody to talk over how she felt, Audrey kept her own counsel, talking to God and herself when she would begin to feel lonely or upset. Actually, after the first shock and the first few days of numbness, Audrey did what she always did. She accepted what had happened to her and went on with her life.

A month went by with little or no changes in their life except that Wesley no longer had his friends over. He didn't quit drinking or playing cards; he just didn't do it at home anymore.

Audrey went to see Dr. Stanley in order to keep peace at home. She hadn't been able to hold anything down for several days, and with Wesley being so contrite and over-cautious with her, it was easier to go see the doctor than fight with him.

"Doctor Stanley, I don't really know what's wrong with me," Audrey said, as she sat down in the doctor's office. "I just keep getting sick, not every day, but almost. Daddy is worried, so here I am."

"Well, Audrey, I'm not too surprised, could just be nerves. You and your Daddy have been through enough lately to cause the strongest person to be a "Nervous Nellie." Let's just have Sally Ann come in here and get you ready. I'll have a look see, and maybe we can figure out what's going on."

"Sally Ann, will you come in here please and take Audrey into the examining room?"

Sally Ann and Audrey walked into the other room, talking as they went. They had gone to school together so this visit was a good opportunity to catch up on all their classmates.

The exam only took a few minutes, and with a couple of pointed questions Dr. Stanley made his diagnosis. "Audrey, I'm pretty sure you are pregnant. I'm truly sorry that this happened. It never even occurred to me to caution you the night I came to see you that this could happen. You've healed very nicely, and I feel certain that you will have a normal pregnancy."

"How can this be? I'm not married. I don't even have a beau. Now Daddy will never be able to forget." Audrey lived on a farm, she knew very well how it could be. They had all been trying to get on with their lives, trying to forget all the hurt. Now that seemed to be impossible, but even now she was thinking about what others would feel and think.

"Thank you, Dr. Stanley, I guess I better go tell Daddy and get it over with." Her eyes were large with unshed moisture, but she wouldn't cry, there was no point. Picking up her purse she walked out the door with her head held high.

* * * *

It took six weeks for the trial to take place. By then it was evident to Doctor Stanley and Audrey that she was pregnant.

Gene, with his lawyer's advice, waived a trial by jury and appeared before the judge. Eugene and his family, Fred, John, Doctor Stanley, Audrey and Wesley were all there.

They were all sworn to tell the truth. Fred, John, and Wesley told what they saw and heard. Basically it was exactly the same story they had told the sheriff back in March.

Sheriff Bailey confirmed his part.

It was Doctor Stanley's story that made the most impression, especially his final comment. "As a result of this attack, Audrey Dickinson is with child. I believe that the child will arrive sometime in November."

Gene's lawyer whispered to him, then with a nod from Gene, which seemed to imply that he was in agreement, the lawyer stood up and addressed the judge. "Your Honor, my client pleads guilty and throws himself on the mercy of the court."

Judge Bennett called a recess, asking Audrey to follow him into his chambers.

He asked her three questions. "Were you forced against your will?"

"Yes."

"Are you pregnant as a result of this attack by Eugene Godwin as Doctor Stanley contends?"

"Yes."

"Do you or would you want to marry Eugene Godwin if it were possible?"

"No!"

With those answers ringing in his ears, Judge Bennett pronounced sentence.

"One year in jail. Doctor Stanley's bill to be paid for service rendered, now and when the baby is born. Five hundred dollars to be paid directly to Audrey Dickinson to help in the support of the said child. Sentence is to be served in the Huntsville prison, with time off for good behavior."

With that they all filed out of the courtroom, except Eugene and his family who said their good-byes before Sheriff Bailey led him away.

Sheriff Bailey heard from Wesley that Ben Godwin brought Audrey $500.00 in small bills a few days later.

"Told her he was sorry, Sheriff, not his place to be cleaning up after Gene." Wesley didn't sound like he was satisfied with the way the judge had handled the situation.

Sheriff Bailey checked on all the participants over the next few months. He wasn't surprised when Gene came home after only six months. Gladys had his first son while he was still in jail, and Audrey was well on her way to having his second child when he came home.

* * * * *

As the months flew by Audrey tried to decide on a name for the baby growing inside her.

One day while walking down by the creek she remembered the afternoon she and Estelle had talked about Billy Bartlett and his mother. The most mysterious boy in school who didn't seem to have a father.

"Billy," she rolled the name around in her mouth and her mind. "Billy, yes, why not? It seems Miss Bartlett and Miss Dickinson might have a lot more in common than I thought."

It didn't occur to her that the baby could even possibly be a girl. It was almost as if she knew from the very beginning that her first child would be a boy.

Billy Hugh Dickinson was born in November of 1929—blonde hair and blue eyes like his mother. From the very beginning he was known as Billy Hugh.

Audrey named him after Billy Bartlett and Hugh after her Uncle Abraham whose complete name was Abraham Hugh Dickinson. As far as Audrey knew he had always signed his name as A.H. Dickinson, but liking the name Hugh, she felt Billy Hugh was a very appropriate name for the newest addition to the Dickinson family. So Billy Hugh it was.

A gift from God you can't refuse.
A gift from man is for you to choose.
Take man's gift or leave it,
God's gift is for keeping.

–Viola Dickinson

CHAPTER TEN

Some days Audrey thought being a mother was the greatest gift she had ever received, and other days she wondered how on earth she had ever become the mother of this beautiful child.

From the very first, Billy Hugh was an easy child to care for. Audrey had plenty of babysitters. Violet was in and out of the house, Purvey had come home for good right before Billy was born, and of course Wesley loved children. The small house became too small for Purvey rather quickly, but there did not seem to be a place for her and Billy Hugh other than to stay with her father.

Audrey was thrilled to have Purvey home, but it just wasn't the same. The talk about his killing Renee continued, and it was a certain fact that none of the neighbors were forgetting who Billy Hugh's daddy was or how he got here. Between the rape, Billy Hugh's birth, and Purvey accidentally killing Renee, it was just too much for Purvey. He was ready to leave Winston County for good and said as much to Audrey.

So it was no surprise to Audrey when Purvey and Lizzie Pruitt got married and decided to move to Haleyville to begin their life together. Purvey had met Lizzie before he was sent away, and she had not forgotten him. Lizzie had even sent a couple notes to Purvey inside Audrey's letters.

With Purvey gone and Wesley on the verge of another marriage, Audrey wanted to leave too. She, like Purvey, was tired of the gossip. When she expressed her desire to move, Lizzie and Purvey made her welcome in their small home, with Lizzie gladly helping her with Billy.

Audrey got a job in a little grocery store. The store being close to Purvey and Lizzie's home made it easy for her to get back and forth to work. She wanted to help with her and Billy Hugh's expenses, although she had not been trained to do anything but keep house and care for children. She really tried hard, but Mr. Swanson didn't seem to be happy with her efforts.

B. J. BROOKS

"Audrey, this store has never been so clean," Mr. Swanson said, "but I really need someone to help more with the customers."

"I know, Mr. Swanson, I'm trying, but they just never seem to be satisfied. If they ask for sugar and you give them sugar they say they want flour. I'm sorry." *It seems like I am always telling someone I'm sorry.*

Early Tuesday morning, after less than a week on the job, Mr. Swanson stopped her between the aisles. As Audrey later told Lizzie, "I was just about to get five pounds of flour off the top shelf for old lady Thompson when Mr. Swanson walked up and grabbed me by the elbow."

He said, "Audrey, I'm sorry, but I am going to have to let you go."

Mr. Swanson had not picked the best time to tell her, as Dr. Watson and his driver were in the store, as well as half a dozen other people, including old lady Thompson, as Audrey referred to her, the town gossip.

Audrey was dumbstruck, but with her head held high she started towards the door, sitting the flour back on the shelf where she had just retrieved it.

"Miss Dickinson. Audrey." Dr. Watson stepped in front of her as she reached the door. "I'm sorry, I didn't mean to overhear, or interfere, but if you don't have another job lined up, I need a housekeeper."

"You do?"

"If you think you might be interested?" Dr. Watson spoke softly, looking at Audrey directly as he waited for her answer.

Audrey knew her choices were limited, so it took only a moment to answer. "Yes sir, I'm interested. I do need a job."

"Well then let's step outside and talk about it." As he was speaking, he opened the front door for her.

"Audrey, this is my driver, Pascal Pratt."

"How do you do, Mr. Pratt?" As she spoke to Pascal, Audrey looked him over. He was tall, about six feet, she thought to herself. Nice looking, she would have to remember everything so she could tell Lizzie. Lizzie loved to hear her stories about the people she came in contact with during the day, and Audrey wasn't above embellishing a little bit just to hear her laugh.

"Miss Dickinson, nice to meet you." Pascal acknowledged the introduction.

"I'll have Pascal pick you up and bring you to my house in the morning, if you will be so kind as to tell him where you live. My housekeeper left me yesterday for parts unknown, and since my wife died, I have depended on her to keep me straight." Doctor Watson was silently congratulating himself on being able to replace Maggie so quickly. Swanson's loss was his gain. Maggie had been his housekeeper for several years, but she was a lousy cook. He just wasn't good at firing people, so it was a blessing in disguise to him for Maggie to leave on her own.

Audrey knew who Doctor Watson was. He was to Haleyville what Doctor Stanley was to Winston County. The only doctor around. She knew Pascal Pratt by sight only. He had been the doctor's driver for about six months. Doctor Watson couldn't see well enough to drive anymore. But his practice kept him on the move, so a driver was the most logical choice.

"Thank you, sir, that would be very nice. I am living with my brother Purvey and his wife Lizzie, over by the saw mill." Those instructions were sufficient for most anyone in Haleyville to find her.

"Good, we will see you first thing in the morning," Doctor Watson told Audrey as he and Pascal re-entered the store to do Dr. Watson's weekly shopping.

Well how 'bout that? Audrey thought. *Fired and hired all in the same day.* She almost skipped on her way home she was so happy. Things were definitely looking up for the Dickinson children.

Lizzie was sweeping the living room floor when Audrey came through the front door. "Audrey, you startled me. I wasn't expecting you until about six. Billy Hugh is on a pallet in the kitchen asleep."

"I'm sorry Lizzie, I didn't mean to scare you. Mr. Swanson fired me. That's why I'm home so early."

"Oh, no! Are you okay?"

"I'm fine. Doc Watson was there and said he needed a housekeeper, so I am going to start there in the morning." Audrey was talking as she picked up some fruit jar lids Billy Hugh had been playing with. Walking on into the bedroom, she took off her work dress.

Lizzie continued to follow Audrey through the house, asking questions as she went from room to room two steps behind her. "I thought Doc Watson had somebody to keep house for him already. Are you going to live over there? What about Billy Hugh?"

"I don't know. He didn't say anything about living there. His housekeeper just up and left yesterday. Doctor Watson said he'd have his driver come over and get me tomorrow. I don't even know what time he will be here." Audrey had made her way into the kitchen to check on Billy Hugh and Lizzie was still talking to her about the new job.

"Oh, Audrey, his driver is so cute. I saw him last week when Billy Hugh and I walked to work with you. He was driving the doctor down the road towards the hospital."

"Lizzie, really!" Audrey thought to herself Lizzie was absolutely right, but she didn't tell her that. Truth was, Audrey wasn't all that crazy about men, at least she didn't think she was. After what happened with Eugene Godwin, she really didn't want to think too much about men.

"Lizzie, isn't he just the cutest thing all curled up asleep with his teddy bear?" Audrey brushed Billy Hugh's hair out of his face and gave him a quick kiss. She adored this child; it was the man-woman thing that it took to get him that was still frightening to her.

"You know he is a sweetheart, I can't wait for me and Purvey to have one just like him."

The next morning, not really knowing what time to expect Pascal, Audrey got up early and helped Lizzie with Purvey's breakfast. The two women prattled on about this and that as they went about the morning chores. Billy Hugh was content to be carried around on his mother's hip.

About nine they heard a car outside and peeking out the window, Lizzie said, "It's him. Oh, Audrey, I told you he was real cute."

Pascal knocked on the door. Lizzie, looking pointedly at Audrey, answered the door just as Pascal was ready to rap again. She almost got swatted on the nose she was so quick to pull the door open.

"Morning, Mrs. Dickinson. I'm here to pick up Miss Audrey."

"Certainly. Come on in." Lizzie let Pascal step through the door, and standing a little to the back and side of him, she winked at Audrey.

Audrey tried not to laugh or smile at Lizzie's antics. "I'm ready, Mr. Pratt. Lizzie, will you watch after Billy Hugh?"

"That's okay, Miss Audrey. Doctor Watson knows all about Billy Hugh, and he said to just bring him along with you. I will bring them home about six ma'am."

That was the beginning, Pascal would pick her up about nine each morning and bring her home about six. Doctor Watson seemed to be very pleased with Audrey, and he even appeared to enjoy the days she brought Billy Hugh along.

Every day she cleaned his house and his office, which was attached to the house. Audrey, being the good cook that she was, cooked his lunch and supper. She even did the laundry.

She enjoyed her days at Doctor Watson's. She also confided in Lizzie that Pascal was really nice too.

In the afternoon Pascal would take her back to Purvey's, and that was a treat also. At nineteen, unmarried, with a small son, it was fun to be riding around town with Pascal. He even took her to Winston county one afternoon to visit Wesley.

Doctor Watson was busy at the hospital and told them to go along. He even came up with something he needed from Doctor Stanley to make it seem like business. Audrey thought that secretly he was very pleased that she was seeing Pascal occasionally. It seemed like he was always looking for a reason to pair them up.

Those trips did not go unnoticed by the gossips in Winston County who had not forgotten Audrey and Billy Hugh. There was even speculation about whether Eugene had truly raped her. "Just look at her settin' up there in that car with that man. I'll bet there's more going on there than meets the eye." Every town has its gossips, and this one was no different. Mary Ellen Curtis could hold her own with the best of them, and she fueled the fire about Pascal and Audrey.

Big blue eyes, strawberry blonde hair,
and good with children.
What more could a man want?
Yep, she's just right.

—Henry White

CHAPTER ELEVEN

Audrey met Henry White at the old Shady Grove Church. She took Billy Hugh to church every Sunday, but this Sunday was special. She had a chance to go to Shady Grove to hear Uncle Abraham. He and Aunt Viola and their children had always been very special. They had been there for her when her own momma died, and their children were her best friends, especially Olivet. She had helped take care of him as a baby and felt a special attachment to him. She was only seven when he was born, but her Aunt Viola had said, "You are just the right size to keep an eye on the baby while I work in the garden." That statement had endeared Viola and Olivet to Audrey.

Henry and the rest of the Barefoot Boys Quartet sang that morning. The quartet was called the Barefoot Boys because they did not wear shoes. They came from a big family, and if one had a good pair of shoes, you could bet that the rest of them didn't. Audrey heard that they mostly sang at church and church events.

She couldn't tell you much about the rest of the group, but she did notice a certain young man with pitch-black hair and very dark, piercing eyes.

After the services, people seemed to hang around just to visit, and this Sunday was no different. All of the Dickinson children came over to see Billy Hugh.

Uncle Abraham pulled Audrey away from the crowd, introducing her to some of his parishioners, one of whom was Paralee White, Henry's mother.

"Hello, Mrs. White, it's very nice to meet you." Audrey, with her direct way of looking at people noticed Paralee was speaking to her but looking at Billy Hugh playing with the other children.

"Nice to meet you too, Miss Dickinson. Your uncle has told me all about you."

Not knowing what to say to that, Audrey was very happy to be interrupted by a loud cry coming from Billy Hugh. He had lost sight of her and didn't seem to like all the strangers.

Audrey didn't remember exactly how it happened, but she found herself standing next to Henry as they were loading up the wagons to go home.

"Howdy, ma'am." Henry was looking at her with the deepest, darkest eyes she had ever seen.

"Good afternoon, Mr. White. Your group sang very well." Audrey really didn't know what to say to the handsome, young man standing beside her, but she enjoyed his very presence and thought to herself that time could slow down for all she cared.

"Thank you, ma'am. Could I see you home from church?" Henry, who was normally shy, seemed to be drawn to Audrey. She had the most beautiful, strawberry blonde hair, which she was wearing in a braid down her back. He liked her friendly ways. She seemed to know everyone. He even noticed she spoke to the children in the same voice that she addressed the adults, not treating them like children as some adults did.

"Thank you, Mr. White."

"Call me, Henry."

"Thank you, Henry, but I am going home with my uncle and from there to my daddy's house. Me and Billy Hugh are going to be staying with him for awhile." It never occurred to her to explain who Billy Hugh was or their relationship. To Audrey he was just Billy Hugh, her son.

"Well it was nice meeting you, ma'am. Maybe I'll see you again sometime." Sometime would be real soon if Henry could do anything about it. He had noticed Billy Hugh. He loved children, so he didn't mind if Audrey had half a dozen. He wasn't planning on courting her children. He just wanted to see more of her.

"Henry, call me Audrey. Ma'am sounds like someone besides me."

Abraham called to her that they were ready to go, so waving Billy's little hand as well as her own, Audrey said good bye to Henry White, for how long she did not know.

Audrey had worked for Doctor Watson for about six months and seemed to really enjoy her job. Living with Lizzie and Purvey was okay; but Lizzie was pregnant and she felt like they needed their space and privacy. Besides that, Wesley had told her he missed her and Billy Hugh, so she decided to move back to Double Springs.

Wesley remarried while Audrey was gone. He married Elizabeth Busby, a widow. Elizabeth didn't have any children, and it was with her blessing that Audrey and Billy Hugh came home to stay. Violet stayed mostly with her grandmother, only occasionally visiting Wesley and Elizabeth.

Audrey was a little surprised the next Saturday evening when she opened the door and found Henry and his brother Bart standing there.

"Good evening, Miss Audrey, we were wondering if your daddy might be home?"

"Yes, Mr. White, I mean Henry. He is here somewhere. Is there anything I can help you with?"

"No, ma'am. We were just wondering if he was home."

"Well, if you fellows will have a seat over there, I will send Billy and Violet to get him." Wesley was back up in the woods somewhere. If Audrey guessed correctly, he was messing with his still and no doubt that sideline was why the White boys were standing at his front door. Audrey was puzzled when they turned her down on her offer to send for Wesley.

"Thank you, Miss Audrey. We will sit awhile, but there's no need to send for him. We have time, don't we, Bart?" Henry looked at Bart with a you-better-not-say-anything-different look.

They sat there for close to two hours. Audrey finished helping with supper, trying to keep Billy Hugh and Violet busy. More than once she offered to send for Wesley, but the offer was declined. They talked some about the weather and the crops that would soon be planted.

Finally Henry stood up and said, "We will come back another time, Miss Audrey. Please tell him we stopped by."

"Certainly." Taken a little by surprise at their leaving without anything, Audrey wondered if Mr. Henry White had been as curious about her as she had been about him. She would have to ask Nora Blanton about him. She thought he and his brother picked cotton for Preacher Blanton sometimes.

* * * * *

Bart really was put out with Henry. They had wasted two hours and still didn't have any shine, and it was Saturday night. "For heavens sake, Henry, what we go over there for if we weren't gonna' get anything?"

"Never mind, Bart, we will stop over at Bud Simpson's. He always has an extra jug or two of Wesley's that he will part with."

Henry had no intention of telling Bart his real reason for visiting the Dickinson home. All week long he had thought about Audrey, and he needed to see her one more time to make sure he had not been day-dreaming about a vision that wasn't real.

Watching her with Violet and Billy Hugh had made Henry's mind up.

Whistling as he and Bart made their way down the road to Bud Simpson's place, Henry said more than once, "Yep, she's just right."

Bart, having no idea what had gotten into Henry, decided to leave well enough alone and just be happy that they were finally on their way to getting what they had set out to get. At least he thought that had been their purpose.

Just as I am
and waiting not.

—Audrey Dickinson

CHAPTER TWELVE

Audrey did ask Nora about Henry and found out he was one of ten children. Seven boys and three girls, Ira, Harry, Bart, John, Bud, Jess, Alice, Lilly, and Mae. Alice had burned to death in a tragic fire as a small child, but the remaining children were healthy, outgoing young men and women. The only problem as Nora saw it was that they were all very dominated by their mother, Paralee. They did not often go against her wishes.

At the moment, one of her wishes was that Henry did not have a lot to do with a certain young lady by the name of Audrey Dickinson. Paralee viewed her as a fallen woman. She chose to ignore how Billy Hugh was conceived, but instead preferred to believe Audrey had taken advantage of Eugene Godwin in some fashion to cause him to rape her.

As these things go, when there is an attraction, a very strong attraction, parent's wishes go unheard.

Henry continued to come over almost daily, using Wesley as an excuse, but in reality spending his time with Audrey and Billy Hugh. They went to church together, which was the social world of the community.

Paralee White took exception to that also and often muttered to her husband, Will, about it.

It was a very warm day for March, and Audrey and Henry had gone to church at Rock Creek, a small Baptist church near Wesley's home. This particular Sunday, they sat close to the back of the church, a two-fold purpose: Billy Hugh sometimes got restless, and they liked the privacy a little more back there. You could whisper quietly during the singing, and the looks from the older generation weren't quite so bold if they had to turn around and look at you.

"Audrey, what ya think about me and you getting married?" Henry leaned over and whispered in her ear.

Audrey had just opened her mouth to join in the singing. They were singing one of her favorite hymns, "Just As I Am." This was one of those old songs she could sing without looking at the songbook, though she held the book open to the proper page just in case Henry wanted to sing too.

"Just as I am and waiting not," Audrey began singing the first verse, with a beautiful, soft, alto voice.

"Is that your answer?" Henry again whispered in her ear.

At that point Audrey collapsed in laughter, dropping the songbook and sitting down hard in the pew. Now that caused a few of those backward looks she and Henry had been concerned about. Laughter in church was unheard of. What on earth could be funny? Church was a serious matter.

Still smiling with laughter in her eyes, Audrey nodded yes. What a proposal, at least she thought that was what it was.

Billy Hugh, thinking this was a fun game promptly fell backwards in the pew trying to imitate his mother. Only in the process he bumped his head and let out a loud yelp. Clamping her hand over Billy's mouth, Audrey and Henry both rushed out the back door, not stopping until they were well away from the church.

"Audrey, I'm sorry I didn't mean to. Well, yes, I did mean to ask you. I just didn't mean to start a ruckus when I asked you. Anyway, will you, I mean do you think we should, do you want to?"

Henry rambled on and on until she stopped him by laying her hand on his arm, and this time she not only nodded but managed to say, "Yes, yes, yes!"

"How 'bout you, Billy Hugh, you want to get married?" Henry turned to look at Billy who wasn't sure if he wanted to keep crying or join in the fun.

Fun won out, and Billy said, "Yes, yes, yes," just like his mother.

The romance blossomed, and in April they were married at Rock Creek Church. A very simple ceremony was performed by Abraham and attended by all the aunts, uncles, and cousins on both sides of the two very large families.

Audrey looked lovely in her pale blue dress with a white collar. She had made it herself from flour sacks she and Viola and Lizzie had saved. They had all bought the same bags of flour in order to get the same material for a dress. This was a joint effort, and they were now saving for Viola, then it would be Lizzie's turn.

Henry thought there could not be a prettier bride anywhere. The blue dress brought out the blue in her eyes, and the strawberry blonde hair all but sparkled hanging in soft curls.

Audrey had scrubbed her head so hard that her scalp turned a bright pink. After that she had curled her hair with tobacco tin strips. These were pieces of tin cut in long strips from the tobacco cans Wesley used. She then wrapped brown paper cut from the grocery bags around the tin to keep from cutting her fingers. Rolling her hair around the long strips, bending them over to hold her hair in place until it dried had been well worth all the trouble. The final product looked very natural, with her hair curling softly around her face.

You couldn't tell who was prouder, Wesley or Henry. Wesley was beaming with pride watching Audrey and Henry say their vows.

After the ceremony there was a dinner on the grounds in celebration of the occasion. Church folks loved to have dinner on the grounds as they called it. The men sat up tables made from sawhorses and large boards. Any occasion was perfect for all the ladies to fix their special fried chicken and fried apple or peach pies, depending on the season and depending on how much they had canned the year before.

Audrey thought it was the most beautiful wedding she had ever seen, and it didn't bother her that they were simply going back to Wesley's house that night.

Wesley had suggested they stay with him until they could find a home of their own. He was happy that Audrey and Henry were married, but he wasn't ready for Audrey to leave. This way she would be in his life a little longer.

They had found a little house several miles away. It needed some fixin' up. Audrey told everyone who would listen. They were going to be able to stay there in return for Henry's working in the fields for their keep. Henry figured he could do that in the evenings after he came home from working at the sawmill and also on Saturday and Sunday. It didn't matter as long as they were together.

They would just have to wait another week or two because the fixin' up included a new roof, but in Audrey's eyes it was just a matter of time until she would be in her own home with Henry and Billy Hugh. So what was a few more days or weeks?

* * * * *

Yes, it was a very simple ceremony that some said should have taken place a lot sooner. One of those was Stella, Bart's wife. Stella kept count and when Audrey started showing all the signs of impending motherhood, she was quite sure that her wedding was a lot later than it should have been.

Others remembered the time Audrey had spent with Pascal Pratt and the car rides. No one outside of Henry and Audrey knew for sure, and they did not tell.

Those girls ain't foolin' me none.
I know a pregnant woman when I see one.
Them boys are plain fools
to be drug around like that.

—Paralee White

CHAPTER THIRTEEN

Several weeks later the newlyweds, along with Bud and Vertie White, Henry's brother and sister-in-law, went to visit Paralee and Will, Henry's parents. Both Vertie and Audrey were in the family way, but they had not told many people.

As they came down the road, Will and Paralee were sitting on the front porch talking, with Paralee doing most of the talking.

"Will, do you think Henry knew Audrey was pregnant when he married her?" Paralee inquired of him.

"Can't rightly say," Will replied. "Ain't asked him."

"Lot of help you are, old man. That boy don't know what he's got hisself in for. That daddy of hers and that little ol' boy. Folks say he's Eugene Godwin's boy, and I know my own eyes tell me she's pregnant. If it ain't Henry's, whose is it? Will, are you listening to me?"

He wasn't, but he nodded his head yes. He was whittling, his favorite pastime. He was making a wooden horse for that "little ol' boy" Paralee was a-fussing about. Will liked Audrey and Billy Hugh. He liked little children. The key word was little, not so big as to be a real bother.

As Paralee was talking, the object of their conversation pulled into the yard in Bud and Vertie's wagon. To Paralee's critical eye, both women looked very pregnant. She vowed to herself to get to the bottom of the possibility on both counts. Today they would both be in her house and these were her boys. She had a few things to say to both young women. After all, they had married into her family and she had a right. Didn't she?

"Hmmmmph," snorted Paralee. "She ain't a-fooling me sittin' in that wagon—probably rather be out a riding the roads with that feller from Haleyville. Mary Ellen told me all about seeing them riding around town just a few months back."

Audrey did not hear Paralee's remarks, but she did catch the look on her face. She turned to help Billy Hugh out of the wagon. *It doesn't matter. What she thinks doesn't matter. Henry loves me, and I will be a good wife!*

As soon as Billy's feet hit the ground, he ran over to where Will was sitting. Billy Hugh had a way with older people. If Paralee would have left the door open, he would have won her over too. But her heart was shut to this one. Not so with Will.

"Well, young Bill White, what brings you over here to see me? It wouldn't be this here little ol' horse I'm a- makin' for you, would it?"

Billy Hugh repeated the new words, "Bill White, Bill White." He had always been called Billy Hugh, and this was something knew. Laughing, he continued to say, "Bill White." Sometimes substituting Bob White for Bill White. Bobwhites he knew about. His daddy whistled for the Bobwhites for him.

Perhaps Will had called him Bill White just to irritate Paralee because of her earlier comments, or maybe he simply was thinking of the similarities of his own name. Whatever the reasons, it stuck. Billy Hugh became Bill White. Legally? No, but those who mattered didn't worry about those who didn't.

Henry was very much in love with Audrey, and it was quite evident that his acceptance of Billy Hugh was equally true. They were, seemingly, a very happy family.

Paralee did not make any headway that day. Billy Hugh, now Bill White, stole the show. By the time she thought up another leading question for the two women, it was too late. They were all climbing in the wagon waving good-bye and calling out their thank yous for such a good supper and a good time. Bill White, asleep in his new daddy's arms, was holding his wooden horse and had no idea he had caused such a stir at the White house.

If today is too tough for you,
then think about yesterday
or tomorrow,
today doesn't last that long.
What's twenty-four hours in a lifetime?

—Suz Hunter

CHAPTER FOURTEEN

"Henry, I think it's time. The pain is a lot worse."

"Okay, Sug, whatcha' want me to do?" Henry was out of his element. He had taken part in his share of birthing with farm animals. But this was Audrey, and he didn't like seeing her in pain.

"I'll be okay for awhile. Just take Billy over to Vertie's, and see if Suz Hunter can come. Get Doc Stanley too. He said he would come when it was time. But, Henry, go get Suz first. If you can't get here in time with Doctor Stanley, then Suz and I will make out okay."

Just then Audrey had another sharp pain. She grabbed Henry's arm and moaned softly.

Henry didn't want to leave her. He never knew he could love anyone like he loved Audrey, and seeing her in pain was more than he thought he could handle. She looked really sick, not like herself at all. He hadn't been around many women when they had babies, actually none. Men weren't allowed. They were always sent outside; to do what, he did not know. He just knew he was supposed to wait someplace until it was over.

He would hurry! "Come on, Billy. Want to go for a ride on old Mac?" It wasn't quite dark yet, so Billy wouldn't be scared. Billy loved to ride on Mac, and going some place with his Daddy was okay with him. "Come on, little fellow, Mac's a waitin'."

* * * * *

Suz wasn't too surprised to see Henry. She had just told Granny Hunter that morning, "Granny it's about time for Audrey to drop that little one." She was carrying real low—a girl for sure in Suz's book. She had gotten to be pretty good at predicting these things. "A girl for sure. Henry will have one of each now," Suz kept talking to Granny as she peeled potatoes for supper.

Just as Suz was about to set the pot of potatoes on the stove, Henry, one of the objects of their conversation, stepped into the kitchen "Suz, Audrey sent me to get you. She says it's time. I'm going to take Billy to Vertie and go after the doctor." Henry was talking way too loud for the small kitchen, as he stood there holding Billy's hand, looking for all the world like a little boy himself.

"Okay, Henry, just leave Billy Hugh here. Vertie looked a little peaked herself this morning. Granny will watch him. Now go on and fetch the doc. I'll head on over there." As Suz talked, she was gathering up her few medical supplies, just in case. She took off her apron, and put on her bonnet. "Somebody go hitch that wagon up! I'm in a hurry!"

Suz's family knew what that meant. She was in great demand as a midwife, and it was nothing for her to leave at all hours of the day or night, just to be on hand in case the doctor didn't make it, which quite often was the case. That didn't bother Suz though. She liked her part in the procedure.

"Billy Hugh, I'm gonna' go help your momma get you a little sister. Now you stay here with Granny Hunter. She'll get you some milk and bread." Suz knew little boys were always hungry. That did the trick. Billy no longer cared that his daddy and Mac had gone off without him.

In less than an hour Suz was there, patting Audrey on the back.

"Let's get this young'un here." Suz began rubbing her legs with alcohol, then her back and even her arms. She had learned over time what seemed to help new mothers in the early stages of labor to relax and let nature take its course.

"It's going to be okay. We have plenty of time." Suz was talking the whole time. Her calm, sure voice also had a very calming effect on Audrey.

There wasn't that much time, because Dora Christine made her appearance moments after Doctor Stanley showed up.

"Just like a man to show up when all the hard part is done," Suz was talking to Audrey as the little, blonde beauty made her way into the world.

Doctor Stanley was used to Suz's comments. They had been in this same situation many times before. So taking no heed to the women now that the baby was safely here, he shook Henry's hand and went on to his next patient.

Christine was born on August 19, 1931. Billy Hugh was just two years and nine months older than his new little sister. Suz had been right, Henry now had a boy and a girl.

Audrey thought Suz was the best. She changed the sheets and helped Audrey clean herself and the baby up. She fluffed the pillows and helped Audrey lay back against them. She then placed Christine in the position she would hold for the next nine months, right next to her mother.

"Thank you, Suz. I couldn't have managed without you." Audrey was looking down at her new daughter, totally absorbed in this new, precious baby. What a difference this birth was from the last.

"No problem, sweetie, my pleasure. You sleep now. I'm going to get Henry fed before he lets folks know the news. Tomorrow you won't get any rest for all the company."

Henry stepped through the door and leaned over his two ladies, planting a kiss on Audrey's forehead. "Sug, you did real good. She's a beauty." He pulled a little hand out of the blanket and counted her little fingers in total awe of this new being.

"Henry, is Billy Hugh okay?"

"Sure Sug, he's with Granny Hunter. Suz insisted. He was gobbling up some cornbread and milk when I left."

"Henry White, get yourself outta here. She needs some rest. That young'un's gonna' be wantin' something to eat in a little while."

"Yes, ma'am," Henry said, as he gave Suz a snappy salute, dancing out the door. He didn't think he had ever been happier.

"That boy's proud, pert near to bustin'."

Audrey smiled as she drifted off to sleep.

Suz was right. Even though new mothers spent close to two weeks mostly in bed right after giving birth, with friends and neighbors pitching in, Audrey still did not get a lot of rest. Christine stayed hungry, and all those folks just had to hold her and look at her and spoil her, beyond belief. Through it all Henry was the very proud papa waiting his turn to hold her, which he did at every opportunity.

Christine was a very docile, loving baby. The only problem was her day in the sun didn't last long enough. Christine was born in August of 1931 and on April 16, 1933, the whole scene was replayed with Harvey, the newest baby arriving.

I thought having a baby
was supposed to be happy time.
Momma never got mad at daddy
when we were born. Did she?

—Bud White

CHAPTER FIFTEEN

A short two weeks later, after the birth of Christine, Suz Hunter's services were again needed by a member of the White family. This time it was Vertie. Bud had married Vertie when she was fourteen, and the babies began to arrive almost immediately. Paralee had been right the day she thought there were two pregnant daughters-in-law.

Vertie and Audrey became fast friends, for Paralee did not think either were what her boys needed in a wife. The day Vertie's labor began, she and Bud were at Audrey and Henry's checking out their new baby, Christine.

"Vertie, you feeling all right?" Audrey looked at her anxiously as Vertie leaned back in the rocking chair holding her stomach.

"Yes, at least I think so. I've been having this sorta' cramp like. It starts in my back and moves around to the front. Doesn't hurt but just for a minute or so, and it goes away. I'll be okay in a minute."

"Vertie, that is a labor pain. You and Bud better get back home so that baby can be born in your own bed." Audrey was sitting up in her bed nursing Christine as she gave Vertie some very sound advice.

Bud decided his discussion with Henry about his garden could wait till next time. He better get Vertie home. Henry having just gone through this with Audrey began giving Bud instructions on going for Suz and then the doctor.

"Sug, I'm gonna' go with Vertie and Bud and lend a hand."

Laughing at Henry and his eagerness to be a help, Audrey just waved at him as he went out the door to help Bud get the wagon ready.

Vertie, feeling better, leaned over the bed and kissed Audrey and Christine. "Audrey, does it hurt much? I'm a little scared."

"Vertie, it hurts something awful, but Suz will help you; and once you hold that new baby, it will seem like nothing at all."

Henry decided to just go get Suz himself and let Bud take care of Vertie, getting her home as soon as possible.

"Why, Henry White, what you doing at my place again so soon?" Suz asked him, grinning because she figured it was Vertie. Hadn't she and Granny just been wondering how much longer before Vertie got around to having that baby?

"Aw, Suz it's not me this time. It's Bud, I mean Vertie. Audrey says you better hurry on this one. She thinks Vertie has been in labor a long time and just didn't know it was labor."

"Lordy me, these young girls just think they're having indigestion from green apples or something. Granny, you hold down the fort. I'm gonna go see for myself what Miss Vertie is up to. Betcha it's a boy." With that, Suz was out the door right behind Henry.

Suz was on her own on this one. Doctor Stanley was in Haleyville and not expected back till late. By the time Suz and Henry got back to Bud's place, Vertie wasn't thinking she was having a little ol' cramp anymore.

Vertie was getting pretty wound up, and Bud's name was dirt, mud, body waste, and worse. Bud just wasn't very well liked at the moment.

"I hate you, Bud White. You are worse than pig shit. Look what you have done to me. Oh, God, it hurts so bad. Bud White get over here. You good for nothing dog crap." A pillow went flying through the air as Suz and Henry came through the door. Bud had gotten Vertie to bed and from the looks of the room, the pillow was the only thing she had left to throw.

Boy, Henry thought, *I'm sure glad Audrey didn't scream at me. Now I know why men folks just find something else to do while women have the babies.*

"Come on, Bud, let's go down to the barn and have a look at that new colt." Henry hoped the barn was far enough away.

"Henry, I didn't know Vertie knew some of those words she called me. Do you think she's ever going to like me again?" Bud looked upset and pretty tired himself—probably from dodging furniture, Henry thought.

"Sure, Bud, she'll like you just fine, as soon as she has the baby to hold. And in a few weeks, she'll let you know how much."

"A few weeks, Henry? You mean I got to listen to this for weeks?"

"No, dummy, I just mean it will be a few weeks before she will want to, you know what I mean. Before she'll want you messing around with her. Hell, Bud, you know what I mean." Blushing, Henry started toward the door.

"Suz, you don't think you are going to need our help do you?" Bud asked as he inched toward the door. The barn sounded pretty good to him too, maybe they would just go a little farther, maybe down in the holler a ways. He had been meaning to show Henry that muscadine vine he had found down there last week. This would certainly be a good time.

"No, boys, you fellows just go on. Vertie and I will be just fine. Won't we, Vertie?"

Vertie was looking at her like the word <u>fine</u> was not in her vocabulary, and personally she thought Bud should stay right here so she could tell him what slime he was. If somebody would hand her something else to throw at him, she would try to be—what was that word again? Oh yeah, she would try to be fine. Fat chance!

Audrey was right. After questioning Vertie, Suz found out, that little cramp had been going on for two days. Sometimes that first one just couldn't make up his or her mind if he or she wanted to come into this world or not.

Suz worked on Vertie for over an hour just trying to get her to relax enough to have the baby. For awhile, Suz was beginning to think this baby would come backwards. She had assisted Doctor Stanley on one or too breach births, but never on her own.

That Vertie was mad at Bud was an understatement. She had decided that if he wanted this baby, he could damn well have it by himself and that, in itself, was the problem. Suz finally figured out that Vertie was trying not to have the baby. Took another hour to convince her that the only way she was going to quit hurting was to just relax and have the baby.

Suz rubbed her down in alcohol and put a cool rag on her forehead, talking all the time she ministered to her. "Okay, Vertie, push. Push hard. That's it, now relax a minute. Okay, here we go again, push. That's it one or two more pushes, and this baby will be here. Bud can have the next one!"

With that, Marshall White made his way into the world. It was a toss up as to who yelled the loudest, and the longest, him or Vertie.

Suz was worn out. Helping Audrey had been easy. Nothing came easy with Vertie. Suz hoped she waited a long time to have any more children, and hopefully Doctor Stanley would do the honors. As a matter of fact, she would personally tell him that when she took

Granny Hunter to see him next week. That man could have this patient as his very own from now on.

Marshall grew up in two households. Vertie and Bud's and Audrey and Henry's. Vertie was unsure of herself and tried to do everything just right for Marshall, so there were many trips to see Audrey to find out what to do for this or that ailment. Although Marshall was a, seemingly, very healthy baby, Vertie thought every burp was an illness for the first month or so until she learned to relax.

Bud had to pay dearly for running out on her as she put it, for she told everyone he was afraid to stay with her and she was brave; but Bud had to run away. She had to be the strong one. Piece of cake this birthing business.

It was hard to tell who was the proudest papa, Bud with his new boy or Henry with his beautiful, little girl.

Paralee wasn't partial to either child, having Vertie and Audrey as their mother didn't particularly endear them to her. But Will was extremely happy. To him it was as good as a set of twins. Two little ones to hold, and Bill White to talk to about the new babies. Those three could spend hours together as long as the little ones didn't need changing. Will definitely appreciated Audrey, Vertie, or Paralee—anyone who was willing to do the dirty deed. Then he would gladly go back to entertaining the little ones.

Henry and Bud dutifully took their families to see Will and Paralee almost every Sunday afternoon. This pleased Will and Paralee both, but for different reasons. Will just enjoyed his boys and the children, but Paralee wanted to see for herself what those women were up to now.

Wesley did not wait for an invitation or a special day to go see Audrey and Henry. Whenever the mood stuck him he would show up, sometimes alone and sometimes with his wife, Elizabeth.

I know God has a mansion for you,
but that's in Heaven.
Here on earth you can at least
have more rooms.

—Henry White

CHAPTER SIXTEEN

With the White family growing by leaps and bounds, Henry decided they needed another room. Christine, being their only girl, needed a room of her own; one that looked like a little girl was in residence. Three boys and one girl were a good start, in Henry's opinion. Actually he would be happy with about six young'uns, he thought, three of each, pretty little girls for Audrey and strong, rough and tumble boys for him. That sounded about right.

He was stepping off the area he wanted to place the new room as Audrey came around the side of the house to see what he was up to. Christine had told her, "Daddy is walking in circles."

"Henry what on earth are you doing?"

"Building a room, Sug, well, actually I'm measuring off an area for another room. Mr. Pickett wants his old barn torn down to make room for his new one—anyway, he said I could have all the lumber if I tore it down." Henry had been working for Mr. Pickett for several weeks, helping him around the farm. The lumber was an extra bonus.

Mr. Picket liked Henry; he was a hard worker and a good family man. Henry talked a lot about his wife and children and all the things he wanted do for his family. It was during one of Henry's planning-for-the-future talks that Mr. Pickett asked him about the barn. The barn in question was only about five years old and in very good condition. It was just too small and setting in the wrong place as far as Mr. Pickett was concerned. To Henry it looked big enough to live in very comfortably by man or beast, but if Mr. Pickett wanted a new barn, Henry wasn't going to argue with him.

Henry planned on enlisting Bart and Bud's help in tearing the barn down and moving the lumber. He would let Billy Hugh and Marshall (Bud and Vertie's oldest boy) help by pulling out the old nails from the boards, and then they would hammer them straight to be used again. A good job to keep two boys out of trouble and busy for several days.

The used nails would add up to big savings for Henry's project. Henry was not one to overlook a chance to save a few pennies that he thought he might spend on some candy for the youn'uns or on a trinket for Audrey.

If all went well, Audrey would have a new room with lots of windows. Audrey loved windows. Maybe he would just step off enough space and make two rooms instead of one. If he made it the full length of the house he could conform to the original lines of the house and have two rooms rather than one. *Oh well, why not,* he thought. *We might need the extra room. Could be we might have a couple more babies than I planned on.*

Henry was so deep in his own thoughts, until he forgot Audrey was still standing there patiently waiting for him to explain what he was up to.

"Just thought you might like a little more space with all these young'uns. That's all."

"Oh, Henry, yes, yes, yes. I would love another room, maybe two with lots of windows."

"Well, Sug, I don't know for sure, I'm trying to figure out how to build it now. It's hard to know how much lumber there will be and how much we will have to buy."

Bart, Bud, and even Jess, Henry's older brother, along with a couple of the neighbors pitched in to help Henry tear the barn down. They were careful to save as much of the materials as they could for future use as they dismantled the barn. Four wagon loads later, everything was sitting on Henry's property rather than Mr. Pickett's. Now the real work would begin. Henry figured it would take about two weeks of hard work to accomplish what he could see in his mind.

The first Saturday in May, Henry began what his brothers called "Henry's barn re-do," their name for his construction project.

Secretly Audrey was calling the whole adventure "Audrey's windows." Henry had agreed that there would be several windows in the front, back, and side. She was going to see if Mr. Johnson had some lacy material in his rolling store the next time he stopped by. All those windows were going to need pretty, white curtains, and she was just the person to make them.

Bart, Jess, and Bud with their wives and children in tow arrived at Henry and Audrey's about eight that morning. They were all in good humor and anxious to get started. The weather looked as if it was a made to order day for building. There was just enough of a breeze to keep everyone comfortable.

Audrey planned a picnic for the helpers. Knowing they would have several people there most of the day, she baked bread for sandwiches and boiled eggs by the dozen to make egg salad. She even baked a ham she had been saving for a special occasion.

Good neighbors and family never came empty-handed, so there were pies and cakes, cold lemonade, and baked sweet potatoes. Plenty for lunch and snacks in-between. Knowing Henry and his brothers liked their coffee strong and hot, she put the coffee on early. The first pot she poured into a metal pitcher, sitting it to the back of the stove to keep warm, and started another pot. Some mornings Henry could drink a whole pot by himself, and she did not want to run out of coffee.

During Henry's salvage project he found four windows in the loft of the barn as he dismantled it. Mr. Picket said he had no use for them, and Henry knew they would make Audrey's day brighter—and all the days to come. So the windows were carefully transported from one farm to the other. Since he had promised Audrey lots of windows, he figured he would have to buy at least two more. The only problem was none of the windows were the same size nor did they match—but since he was building these rooms to suit no one but Audrey he would put those he would buy on the front of the house. The other four windows would go on the side and back of the rooms. Henry knew Audrey would love all the windows when the rooms were finished.

That first weekend they were able to lay the floor and put up two walls. Henry used the boards from the loft for the flooring since it had been exposed to the weather the least. Audrey was constantly sweeping up wood chips and picking up bent nails, but it was a labor of love that she did not mind. She used that time to plan how she would place her furniture when the rooms were finished.

"Maybe I'll have enough room to put my old rocker in the bedroom. It would be nice to rock the baby during the night without going into the other room."

Vertie and Audrey kept up a running conversation about what could or could not be done with the new rooms while they kept the children out of the way and the men full of food and hot coffee.

Henry worked on the rooms every free moment he had between his various other jobs. On the weekends Bart, Bud, or Jess would come

over and lend a hand. Audrey and their wives spent their time mend-
ing and sewing. There was never idle time to daydream, but always
time to visit and share while their nimble fingers finished one project
after another.

Marshall spent the week with Billy Hugh. They diligently pulled
out the old tenpenny nails from the boards, hammering them straight
again for future use whenever possible. The nails that were too old or
too bent they threw in a bucket. Old Josh down the road would give
them a nickel for a bucket of nails. Nobody ever thought to ask what
he wanted them for, but Billy secretly thought it had something to do
with fishing. Old Josh could always catch a batch of catfish when everyone else complained that the fish just weren't biting.

Once the walls were up and the roof in place, Henry installed the
windows. When he first brought the windows home, he leaned them
up against the house for Audrey to admire. Her first look caused her to
shake her head. She wanted to laugh; they were such an odd assort-
ment. One was octagon shaped. Two were long, and one was a very
large square. She could not imagine how Henry would be able to make
the windows work, or look right in the new rooms. She would not hurt
his feelings in any way, for she knew the windows were for her and not
many men would go to the trouble Henry had just for a smile. So a
smile he got, and a hug too just for good measure.

The finished product, however, was beautiful in Audrey's eyes.
There were two windows on the front of the house matching the three
others on the front. As it turned out Henry did not have to buy two
windows. They had attached the new rooms on the east side of the
house coming off the living room and kitchen. After he removed the
original windows from those two rooms, putting doors in their place, he
used the windows he had removed for the front portion of the addition
he was making. The large square window Henry put on the back of the
room facing the back yard. He put the octagon window in between the
two long windows in the front room of the two rooms facing the side.
To keep the back bedroom from being so dark Henry purchased
another window for the side. Audrey's rooms had a total of seven
windows between the two rooms.

The completed rooms were just what Henry had been seeing in his
mind, and the smile on Audrey's face was all it took to make all the
nights and days of hard work worth it.

Audrey looked like Christmas and every other holiday wrapped in to one. She was so pleased she danced around the room with her broom until Henry handed the broom to Billy Hugh and took its place.

They moved their bedroom into the room with the octagon window, that same day, and put Christine into the new room adjacent to theirs. The younger boys, Harvey and Dempsey were moved from the back bedroom on the other side of the house into their parents old room, leaving Billy with a room to himself on the back of the house.

A home that Audrey was very proud of had emerged from "Henry's barn re-do", but their room was always referred to as "Audrey's windows" for it was her desire for more windows that had given Henry the nudge to build the rooms to begin with.

This old place ain't much,
but I was a-plannin'
on leavin' it to you children
when I was gone.

—Wesley Dickinson

CHAPTER SEVENTEEN

Although Audrey knew it was time for her fifth child to be born, she was not ready to quietly stay home and give birth to another child. She had urged Henry and the children to get ready, for they were going to Wesley's home to spend the day and have dinner with Wesley and Elizabeth.

Today being a beautiful, crisp, clear day made the short trip even more special. Wesley wanted Audrey and Purvey and their families to come for a visit. "A small family reunion," he had said. Purvey, Lizzie, Henry, Audrey, and all the children.

Elizabeth had been cooking for two days. An after Thanksgiving feast that could have fed an army. They had all eaten their fill twice, and Wesley still had not made any move to tell them why he had felt the need for a "small family reunion."

I guess I know him too well, Audrey thought to herself. *Daddy never does anything without a purpose or reason.* But for the life of her, Audrey could not figure out what was on his mind this time.

"Oh, that wasn't what I thought it was, I hope." Audrey had just felt what to her might have possibly been the very beginnings of labor. "Darn, I am not ready for this. Not now—not just yet." Still talking to herself, Audrey walked out on the porch.

Wesley and Henry had gone outside to have a smoke and wait on the women folk to clean up the kitchen. They were sitting in rockers on the porch watching the little ones play in the yard, talking about gardens and chickens. They did not see Audrey come up behind Henry.

"Henry, know what I been thinking?" Wesley leaned back in his chair as he spoke to Henry.

"Can't say that I do, Wesley."

"Well, me and Elizabeth been thinking about sellin' off some of that bottom land behind the barn. Been wantin' to talk to you children about it."

Henry became aware of Audrey when she squeezed his shoulder. Looking up at her he winked. Wesley had finally said what was on his mind.

"Daddy, you don't have to ask me or Purvey either about selling what is yours to sell."

Wesley was so startled when he heard Audrey's voice that he almost fell over. Henry reached out to steady him before his chair toppled off the porch.

"Well, uh, Audrey, I was just a-supposin'. Didn't want to do nothing without first talking to you and Purvey. This place ain't much but I always was planning on leaving it to the two of you when I passed on."

"Daddy, you aren't going no where anytime soon. If you want to sell some land then you should." Audrey squeezed Henry's shoulder. Squeezing a little harder when the second, what just might be a labor pain, hit her. She wasn't ready to call this discomfort labor pains just yet. *Probably just ate too much of Elizabeth's good cooking*, she thought to herself.

"Sug, you okay?" Henry spoke quietly hoping Wesley did not hear him and get concerned.

Audrey nodded as she put her finger to her lip in a shushing motion.

"Daddy, that is really sweet of you to think about mine and Purvey's feelings, but really, you and Elizabeth do whatever you want to with this place."

Purvey walked up on the porch from the yard where he had been taking turns swinging Harvey and Dempsey by their arms. "Did I hear my name mentioned?"

"Purvey, Daddy and Elizabeth are thinking about selling some of that bottom land behind the barn."

"Just thinking about it, son, just thinking about it," Wesley interjected, interrupting Audrey.

"Well, whatcha' waitin' on, Daddy? If you want to sell it then sell it." Purvey, like Audrey, could not see what it had to do with him.

"Well, son, I was just wanting to make sure it was all right with you and Audrey before I decided for sure to sell."

"Well, Daddy, it's fine with me and don't know why you would want me to say so. How 'bout you Audrey? Is it okay with you if Daddy just thinks about selling this bottom land of his?" Purvey was grinning when he turned to question Audrey.

Laughing as she grabbed her stomach leaning forward, Audrey wasn't quiet sure if she wanted to cry or laugh. That was definitely a pain.

Looking up at Henry, Audrey, still laughing but with tears streaming down her face said, "We better be going home Henry. I can tell Daddy needs some peace and quiet to do his thinking."

Henry, putting his arm around Audrey, whispered in her ear, "Is it time?"

Audrey nodded her head and whispered back. "Let's get out of here before Daddy figures out what's up."

Audrey and Henry were almost home when her labor decided to get difficult, and when her water broke she began to think about having a baby in the wagon.

"Henry, you better hurry or this baby is going to be born alongside the road." Audrey was laughing when she said that, but laughter or not, this was beginning to look serious.

"We're a lot closer to Suz's place then we are home. Want to just go there?" Audrey, well into another pain, just nodded her head.

Hazel Marie White, named after Audrey's favorite schoolteacher, joined the White family very quickly at Suz Hunter's home in Suz's very own bed.

Since Marie decided to come a few days early, she spent the first week of her life in the Hunter household rather than her own. What a turn around. Suz, who was accustomed to making unexpected trips to help deliver babies, was taken by surprise at this turn of events, with her patient coming to her.

Marie was the first baby she had delivered in her own home. She and Granny Hunter rose to the occasion, however, and made Audrey and Marie very welcome, while Henry took the other children and went on home for the rest of the night, arriving back at Suz's at the crack of dawn to welcome the newest child to the family.

"Oh, Henry, Daddy is going to love this. You better get word to him as soon as possible. I don't want him to spend too much time thinking about selling his land. Better he should have a new granddaughter to think about." Henry was holding Audrey's hand while he looked over the little bundle she was holding. They were still laughing about Wesley and his small reunion to discuss selling his land.

"I'll take a trip back over to see Wesley later today, Sug. You get some rest. Most likely Wesley will want to come see for himself. I know Christine can hardly wait to see her, she is going to love having a little sister around. I think she is plum tired of so many boys."

"Henry I'm so glad we added on to the house—now Christine will have someone to share her room, and she won't be lonesome."

Henry's new rooms got lots of use. Less than two years after Marie's birth, Charles Peyton White, named after Doctor Stanley, was born. Once again the rooms, or at least the occupants, were moved around. Harvey moved in with Billy. Dempsey and Charles shared a room as well as a bed as did the other children.

Henry had his six young'uns but not in the right numbers that he had requested. He now had four boys and two girls, but in December of 1941 Audrey presented him with another fair-haired beauty.

Letting the older children name her was a big mistake as an argument started that was days in the resolving. Billy was determined she should be named Crystal. That was his very favorite name. Christine liked the name Yvonne and thought that would be the very best name for a new little sister. Audrey wanted to name her Reba, so this tiny, little girl became Reba Crystal Yvonne, in order to pacify everyone. She became the latest darling of her older brothers and sisters.

Jesus made wine from water.
I just changed his recipe
a little bit to
make my shine.

—Wesley Dickinson

CHAPTER EIGHTEEN

Uncle Monroe was coming for a visit. This time it just wasn't one of Audrey's "knowings," but a fact. Audrey had received a letter. Although it wasn't long, it stated all the facts she needed.

> Dear Audrey, Henry, children:
> Will be by to see you for a short visit Saturday about noon.
> Love,
> Monroe

The letter was signed with a large <u>M</u> and the rest of the letters scribbled in Uncle Monroe's familiar style.

"Henry, Henry!" Audrey was so excited she almost tripped over Shep, the dog. She was trying to reach Henry, who had his head stuck under the hood of the truck. He and Harvey had been tinkering around on that old thing all afternoon. It had quit running the day before when Henry had decided to ride into town to pick up a few groceries, and now every time they tried to start it up there was a grinding noise.

"Henry, are you listening to me? Uncle Monroe is coming for a visit. He will be here this Saturday, day after tomorrow, Henry."

"Sure, Sug, I'm listening. Harvey turn it over again, I think I've found the problem."

Harvey climbed into the truck. Holding on to the steering wheel real tight, stretching his full length, he managed to reach his foot to the floorboard to hit the gas, turning the key with his free hand. Unlike the other ten times, it sounded like the old truck would finally start this time.

"Henry, you are not listening to me. I am trying to tell you Uncle Monroe is coming for a visit."

"That's it Harvey. You hear that?" As he was talking to Harvey, Henry was jiggling spark plug wires and various other things under the hood. He was no mechanic but had a sixth sense about wiring and such; and sure enough, he moved just the right wire, and the truck came to life.

"Henry?"

"Yeah, Sug, I heard you. Uncle Monroe is coming for a visit. Just sit tight. Me and Harvey are going to take this thing for a spin, and I will be right back; and then you can read me his letter." Henry jumped into the truck. Moving Harvey over to the passenger side, he revved up the engine.

Audrey just shook her head as they wheeled out of the yard. She had to find someone to share her news with. It was then that she remembered Christine was in her room primping in front of the mirror. Chris was always trying new hairstyles, as young as she was, Chris had a huge interest in clothes and hairstyles.

Running up the steps into the house, Audrey could still hear the old truck as it struggled up the hill headed towards town. "Darn, I wanted to tell him to go by and tell Daddy Uncle Monroe was coming."

"Chris, guess what?"

"I know, Momma, I could hear you telling Daddy, Uncle Monroe is coming." Chris was sitting on the stool in front of Audrey's dresser trying to fix her hair this way and that while Marie held Reba and sat on the bed watching her.

"How long will he stay, Momma?" Marie wanted to know; not that it would make any difference. She loved it when they had company.

"Oh, you know Uncle Monroe, could be two weeks or two days."

"Will he bring his kids?" Uncle Monroe's kids were his grand-children. He and Dealey had their oldest boy's two children most of the time.

"I suppose so. His letter really didn't say."

"Chris, we've got to get started. This house is a mess, and we need to cook and we better wash again tomorrow and—" Audrey went on and on with her "we need to do this and that," list until it was finally the big day.

"Thank goodness, it is Saturday," said Chris. "Momma has about worked me to death."

Just like his letter said, about noon, Uncle Monroe pulled into the yard. He definitely did not come alone. They had stopped on the other side of town and picked up Wesley and Elizabeth. His own wife

Dealey was with him along with their two grandchildren.

Audrey had just put the finishing touches on the noonday meal when she heard all the noise from the front of the house. "Chris, they are here. Hurry up and set the table." Pulling her apron off, she started out the front door.

"Uncle Monroe, Aunt Dealey. It is so good to see you."

"You too, Audrey. My goodness these young'uns get bigger every time I see them, or is there just more of them?"

While he talked he shook Henry's hand and hugged Audrey, and then he began hugging one child after another until even he had lost count.

"Y'all, come on in. Audrey and Chris have dinner on the table." Henry was maneuvering everyone toward the house. He couldn't wait to eat. Seemed to him Audrey and Chris had cooked all week, but he didn't remember eating any of the stuff he had smelled in the preparation stages. They good-naturedly shuffled and pushed each other trying to get to the table first.

When Audrey asked who would say the blessing, both Monroe and Wesley answered in unison, "Abraham can," then laughed out loud at themselves.

Lacking Uncle Abraham to do the honors and knowing Henry would not, Audrey quickly said, "Lord bless this food and forgive these two of their trespasses, amen."

That brought another round of laughter with a flurry of plates being passed up and down the long table for this or that to be placed on them. Mashed potatoes, fried chicken, squash, okra, fresh tomatoes, fried pies, corn bread, and biscuits. Audrey and Chris had made a little bit of everything, finishing off with the boys making homemade ice cream to be served with chocolate cake.

The afternoon passed way too fast. About four o'clock, Vertie, Bud, and their children drove up. Getting out of the car, Vertie said to Audrey, "I hope you don't mind, but Henry told Bud your Uncle Monroe was coming, and we couldn't resist. I brought chicken and dumplings and a couple of pies."

Behind Vertie and Bud the Cagles pulled in and the Hunter family —all bringing pots and pans full of food.

Audrey knew this many people would not fit in her small house or kitchen, but Henry and Bud were ahead of her and had begun setting up tables under the trees. Just when she thought there wasn't room for one more man, woman, or child, the Wilson family pulled up, getting out of their car with a variety of musical instruments.

Then Purvey and Lizzie and their two children drove into the yard. Audrey did not see Lizzie and Purvey nearly often enough. She was very pleased they had come and was mad at herself for not inviting them.

The usual comment was, "We heard Monroe was coming. Hope you don't mind if we just showed up." Evidently Henry and Harvey's little trip to test the truck had been very useful in notifying the whole community that Uncle Monroe was coming.

The tables were full of food, and it certainly did not go to waste. A lot of good-natured fun and laughter went on, and at the first sign of dusk, Uncle Monroe pulled out his guitar and fiddle. Harvey made a beeline for the house, coming back with an old guitar Uncle Monroe had given him a couple of years back.

Harvey would practice down at the barn thinking no one could see or hear him. Audrey knew he, of all her children, seemed to have some musical talent, for she had often paused to listen to him practice.

Monroe settled in a rocker with Harvey sitting on the top step of the porch. They began slowly to warm up, and before long Monroe was strumming and singing. The Wilson family joined in with their various instruments. There was even an old washtub turned upside down that was periodically being thumped by Granny Hunter.

The women were visiting in the house, trying to catch up on all the family, who had seen who last and what they were doing. Soon the music began to vibrate through the house, and since it sounded like fun, they decided to join the men on the front porch.

Henry's foot was tapping to the music, and pretty soon he was up doing the Alabama shuffle. Audrey couldn't stand it any longer; so she joined him, and they danced across the front yard.

Harvey was doing his best to keep up with Uncle Monroe and was doing a pretty good job of it, but when Monroe switched to the fiddle, Harvey gave up and just watched. By now the porch was empty except for Harvey, Monroe, and the Wilson family and, of course, Granny Hunter, but the yard was full. Some of the closest neighbors had slipped over to join in the fun.

Wesley and the men kept going around to the side of the house. Audrey was keeping her eye on her boys and Henry too, to make sure they didn't take that little trip. Henry got happier and happier and danced more and more with a few drinks. Right now he was singing and dancing around with Marie, singing along with Monroe and the Wilson family at the top of his lungs. Bud wasn't in much better shape. Vertie was going to skin him alive if he didn't quit twirling her around.

Wesley still made his home brew and Audrey knew he had probably brought a supply with him, unbeknownst to Monroe. She knew what they were up to but decided to ignore them and just have a good time.

Monroe played on and on with this one and that one joining him in a song. Finally he played "Amazing Grace" and sang the most beautiful rendition Audrey thought she had ever heard.

Earlier in the evening, one after another the smaller children began to fall asleep and were carried into the house and put to bed. Pallets with sleeping children were everywhere. You could not walk for sleeping children.

As the evening wore on, one family after another began loading up their cars. First they gathered up all the empty pots and pans, then they began searching through the sleeping children for theirs, laughing and talking about what fun it was when Monroe came for a visit. There was even talk of how many children might just be left behind and what if they got home with the wrong one, or one too many.

About midnight Audrey asked if anyone wanted to go to bed. "No, Audrey, it has been wonderful; but we are going on home with Wesley and Elizabeth tonight. Tomorrow we are going to head on over to Arkansas. Dealey wants to go see some cousins over there."

Sitting in the swing on the empty porch that held so many just a few hours earlier, Audrey turned toward Henry and asked "Henry, wasn't it just too wonderful?" Audrey was still full of the visit, and this was about the tenth time she had asked Henry if he had enjoyed the evening as much as she had.

"Sug, it was great." Henry replied, stifling a yawn. He was trying to close up the house and get Audrey to bed. It had been a long day.

"Oh, Henry, just go onto bed. I am going to sit here a minute and think about the day." Audrey wanted to remember every detail and remember every word she had heard about the Dickinson family. They were all well, happy, and busy; and it was so good to get news.

"Okay, Sug, don't stay up too long. I miss you when you aren't beside me in bed." Having said that, Henry leaned over and kissed her on the forehead, murmuring, "Good night."

We aren't moving away silly,
we're moving about a mile
up the road.

—Lizzie Dickinson

CHAPTER NINETEEN

After Monroe's visit, Audrey was more homesick than ever. The emotions she was feeling were hard to put into words. Having the family there just one day left her feeling empty after they went home.

Lizzie and Purvey's visit was short, and with so many people there, she did not get to visit with them nearly long enough. Audrey confided in Henry her desire to see more of her family.

"I know it seems silly, but I really miss Purvey and Lizzie. It seems like we never see each other."

"Well, Sug, why don't you just invite them over for a visit. Haleyville isn't that far away. Maybe they would come for a couple of days."

"Henry, would you mind?" Audrey looked at Henry as she asked her question, but her mind was already busy thinking of all the things she would do, if indeed, they could come for a visit.

"Of course not. I like seeing Purvey too."

Giving him a hug, Audrey started searching for a pencil and paper. She would write them today and see if they would come. Taking a clothespin, she attached four cents for postage and sent Charles to the mailbox. Taking her cue from Monroe, she had written two short sentences:

Dear Purvey and Lizzie,
I miss you both so much.
Please come for a visit.
Love, your sister,
Audrey

With her letter in the mail, Audrey decided to wash curtains and windows—anything to stay busy. Otherwise, she would be watching for the postman, even though she knew it would be a week or more before she got an answer.

"Christine, help me rearrange this furniture. I'm sick of the couch in the middle of the floor. Let's move it under the window."

"There, that's better. Don't you think so?" Not even waiting for Chris to answer, Audrey started shoving the rocker closer to the fireplace.

It seemed to Chris they did this every week, or at least every time Audrey thought company was coming, but she enjoyed a change herself. So Chris moved the small table and lamp to the other side of the chair. Grinning, she looked at her mother and said, "There, that's better. Don't you think so?"

Audrey laughed and gave Chris a hug. These moments with Chris were far and few between. They were seldom alone, and the troubles of life and family weighed them down most of the time when they were given time alone.

Audrey knew in her heart that Purvey would not refuse her, so she began preparing for their visit. She and Chris churned butter in the old churn that had belonged to Selah and talked about the visit that Audrey knew would come to pass.

"We can make ice cream. You know how much Uncle Purvey likes your ice cream," Chris said as she brought the paddle up and down in the churn.

"Yes, and I will roast some peanuts; Purvey loves my roasted peanuts."

The butter was so stiff that even though Audrey and Chris took turns it was almost impossible to push the paddle up and down any longer.

"Time to take it up?"

"Yes, and put some in that pretty butter dish Belzie gave me for my birthday. I never get a chance to use that thing." On Audrey's last birthday, Belzie Blanton had stopped by and presented her with a beautiful, blue butter dish. She was very touched by Belzie's thoughtfulness.

Audrey was collecting dishes that came in oatmeal boxes, but so far she had not gotten a butter dish and had mentioned it one Sunday at church. She had not even remembered Belzie's being in the group of women who were discussing their various collections. Quaker Oats and a couple other companies had several dinner patterns inside or attached to their products to get the ladies to buy their brand.

Most of Audrey's dishes were hand-me-downs and mismatched patterns; but recently she had discovered lots of ways to use oats, so she had a good start on her first set of real dishes.

"Chris, now we can finally show off our dishes."

Chris poured up the butter and patted it in a round circle in a bowl, except for the portion she fashioned to fit the blue butter dish that Audrey had spoken of. She took the tines of a fork and fashioned little flowers on the top of the butter. Then she walked down to the spring-house and placed it in a wash-tub that was setting in the cool spring water. An underground well came up near their house, and Henry had built a little covering around it. There they kept all the items that needed to be kept cool.

Next year they were getting a refrigerator. The kind that you just plugged in. They had an icebox now but did not always have ice to put in it, so the spring house worked just fine for them.

Food did not last long enough in the White household to worry about preserving it. Meats were just salted down and kept in the smokehouse. Mostly they ate chicken and fish. Pork and beef were plentiful in the fall months, but during the summer, vegetables were the daily fare with meat on Sunday or when they had company.

Purvey's note finally arrived. They would be there late Friday night and would not have to go home until Sunday afternoon. He also stated he had a surprise for Audrey, one she would like.

"Henry, Purvey will be here Friday night. I can hardly wait. I don't think I'm going to tell Daddy till Saturday, so I can have him to myself just one night."

"Thought so," Henry said. A man of few words, he did not doubt for a minute that Purvey would say no to Audrey's request. Those two were always close.

* * * * *

Henry and Audrey were sitting in the swing gently rocking Reba back and forth. The other children had gone on to bed, too tired to wait up for Purvey and Lizzie. Reba had been suffering with an upset stomach so she had not settled in as easily as the others.

"Henry, I think she's asleep now. I'll just slip her into bed. What time is it anyway? Shouldn't they be here by now?"

"Sug, it is ten minutes later than when you asked awhile ago." Henry put his foot on the floor and stopped the swing so Audrey could stand up with Reba in her arms. He turned to look up the road and sure enough he could see headlights up towards the Blanton home. "I think I see them, put Reba down and come on back out. I'm sure they are gonna want to visit a bit."

Audrey tiptoed through the house hoping she would not wake up the other children, and at the same time trying to hurry so she could be on the porch to welcome her brother.

"Lizzie! Purvey! I am so glad you've come." Audrey was waving and talking to them long before the car even came to a full stop.

After lots of hugging and shoulder patting, they all made it to the front porch, sitting in rockers and in the swing. Audrey was content to just be with the two of them, not caring if she spoke or not.

"Well, Audrey, aren't you just a little bit curious about my surprise?"

"Yes, of course, I am, only I got so excited about seeing you that I forgot to ask. So, what is your surprise?" Audrey stopped the slow movement of the swing so she could hear him above the squeaking.

"Lizzie and me are moving."

"Oh, no, Purvey, you live so far away now, I don't get to see you nearly often enough." Audrey thought she would cry at the very thought of her two favorite people moving farther away. Purvey was laughing, and Lizzie was busy patting Audrey on the back in a consoling manner.

"What's so funny?"

"We aren't moving farther away, silly, we're moving about a mile up the road from you!"

"That's right," Lizzie said. "Purvey found a job in Double Springs, and we were going to write and tell you as soon as all our plans were made. Then we got your letter and decided to just tell you in person."

"Oh, Lizzie, I am so glad!" Audrey looked at Henry and asked, "Did you know?"

"Not for sure. Wesley told me that there might be a possibility, but I didn't want to get your hopes up."

The weekend passed much too quickly for Audrey. She and Purvey had taken a long walk in the woods talking about old times, their childhood, Renee and Wesley. They both liked Elizabeth a lot and were glad Wesley had married again.

Purvey wanted to know how Audrey was feeling. Several weeks back she had a miscarriage, and though she was sad about it, she truly was not ready for another child. Reba wasn't out of diapers, and it would be nice to have one child potty trained before another one made an appearance.

As they pulled out of the yard late Sunday afternoon, the only thing that kept Audrey from crying was knowing it would be less than a month when she would see them again—and with them so close she could walk over anytime she wanted. A mile was nothing.

Purvey said they were going to rent the old Hamilton place. If you went through the woods and crossed over the Washborne Creek, then it really wasn't even a mile. The Washborne boys had built a bridge across the creek, making it even easier to go the back way.

Every child is a gift from God.
Don't ever think he has
lost count — he knows
exactly how many you need.

—Suz Hunter

CHAPTER TWENTY

Audrey knew she was pregnant again. She and Henry had tried to be careful, but after Reba was born she had miscarried a baby. She had been pregnant for the eighth time only six weeks after giving birth to Reba. Doctor Stanley said it was just too soon and her body had not been ready for the baby.

Audrey had talked it over with Purvey; for even though she was not planning on another child so soon, she felt the loss.

Now she was pregnant again. It was 1943, and Reba was not yet two. She was not ready to tell Henry about the new baby, for he too had been disappointed when she miscarried. Henry loved all babies, and it didn't seem to matter to him that they already had a family of seven.

Billy was fourteen; then Christine at eleven was such a big help; Harvey was ten; and Dempsey, whose birth had been so difficult, was eight; then there was their little school teacher, Marie who was only a year and nine months younger than Dempsey. There, again, they had tried to be careful. Marie had just turned seven, with Charles four and Reba who would turn two in December. A very big family,

Audrey decided she would wait till Christmas to tell Henry about the baby; after all she was only a few weeks along. This baby would not be born until late June or early July.

Purvey and Lizzie had moved closer almost a year ago now, and it was so good to visit back and forth. During the summer she and Lizzie would meet at the creek and let their children play in the warm, summer sun, swimming and playing in the water. It entertained the children plus served as their bath for that day.

Often taking a basket lunch, the two of them would sit in the shade of an old, oak tree, doing their hand sewing and watching the children splash around in the creek. In places it wasn't very deep at all. It was very peaceful down by the creek.

Lizzie and Purvey had three children, Jr., George, and Mary. They thought the larger White clan was a lot of fun, so many children to play with.

Now it was almost Christmas and the weather was much colder. Remembering summer days and hot sunshine was all that was keeping Audrey warm today.

She wished she had some peanuts to roast and could sit around the fire and eat them. Maybe it was just a craving caused from this new life growing within her. Purvey had promised to bring her some peanuts but hadn't been to see her in several weeks now. Lizzie said he was working long hours in the sawmill.

Someone was knocking on the door. That was strange. Between children and dogs very few people got as far as the door before Audrey knew someone was around. But the children had gone with Henry, and she had been daydreaming. Maybe the dogs had barked and she had not heard them.

Audrey walked over to the door. "Lizzie, what are you doing here? I didn't hear you come up." As she was welcoming Lizzie, Audrey was looking around her to see how she had arrived. She did not see a car or buggy.

"I walked down by the road. Have you seen Purvey? He left early this morning riding our old mule; he was bringing you some peanuts."

"Oh Lizzie, I have just been sitting here a wishing I had some to roast, but I haven't seen him. When did you say he left coming this way?"

"That's so strange. I thought he would be back home by now. It was so damp in the woods from that last rain that I didn't want to come through there, but I know that is the way he came. I was out back hanging up clothes when he left. Audrey, I'm so worried; that isn't like Purvey at all. You know he always does what he says he will, and he said he would be back by noon. Audrey, it is almost four o'clock now." Lizzie's voice was starting to crack as she tried to keep from crying.

"Lizzie, please don't worry; surely he is okay. Maybe the creek was higher than he thought, and he went on further down to cross over. He might have stopped to talk with old man Cagle over the ridge there. You know how long that old man can talk."

"Come on in here and get warm. I'll heat us up a cup of coffee. Purvey will probably show up any minute now, and he can have some coffee with us." She led Lizzie further into the room as she continued. "Henry will be back from town soon, and we will send him and the boys to look for Purvey, if he isn't here by then."

Lizzie came on in and sat close to the fireplace. She was shivering from fear or from cold, or both. She just couldn't understand why he hadn't come home. "Audrey, he knew my mother and father were coming for a visit. They are here now, and he knew they were coming." Lizzie, who never repeated herself was still talking as Audrey came back with the coffee.

"I didn't want Mother to worry, so I asked her to stay with the children while I walked over to hurry Purvey up. At first I thought you weren't home and he was waiting on you." She had fully expected to see him sitting patiently on the porch waiting on the family to return. She had seen Henry and the children go by their house earlier in the day. Audrey could have been with him.

Now that she was here, and Purvey wasn't, she was really worried. What could have happened?

Audrey was back with the coffee and a quilt, which she wrapped around Lizzie. "Here Lizzie, drink this. It will warm you up. I think I hear that old truck of ours." Leaving Lizzie by the fire Audrey walked out on the porch to greet Henry and the children.

"Hi, Sug, we're back." Henry was getting out of the truck handing a bag of groceries to each child. Harvey and Dempsey had their arms full and were halfway up the steps when Audrey stepped out into the yard. Chris was holding Reba, and Marie was bouncing around all over the place, with candy smeared on her face. Marie had a sweet tooth that was uncontrollable.

Audrey was all set to fuss at Henry about Marie and the candy when she remembered Lizzie was in the house. "Henry, something is wrong with Purvey. Lizzie is here, and she said he left sometime this morning on their old mule coming over here. Henry, Purvey hasn't been here."

"Poor Lizzie, I bet she is worried sick. Let's get these groceries in the house, and the boys and I will go look for him." Henry went back to the truck, handing Harvey and Dempsey another bag of groceries, then helping Charles down from the bed of the truck. Charles had been scooting the bags to the edge for the other boys to lift down and take in the house.

"Billy went home with Bud and Vertie to stay a couple of days, I'll ride over and get him Monday. They were at the store, and he and Marshall cooked up a hunting trip." Henry saw Audrey mentally counting heads and thought he better explain why he had left with seven and he'd come home with six. At least that took her mind off Marie and the candy. He knew he would catch it for that, but he could not resist giving her candy, and the Hamilton's were just as bad. They owned the grocery in Double Springs, and Marie was one of their favorites.

After talking to Lizzie, Henry decided he better get someone besides his boys to help him look. It was going to be dark soon, and he might need some help getting Purvey home if he were hurt. A man could take a tumble in the woods, breaking a leg or arm, making it difficult to move quickly without help.

He sent Harvey up towards the Blanton's, and Dempsey down towards the Cagles with instructions to "Tell the men of the family to bring lanterns, Purvey Dickinson is lost in the woods between his place and ours."

In less than an hour, seven men started out across the back yard heading into the woods to look for Purvey. Lanterns were throwing an eerie light around them. Although it was barely dusk, they had taken time to light their lanterns. They knew once they entered the woods darkness would fall quickly.

Audrey and Lizzie stood in the open doorway, watching as the lights moved into the woods. Lizzie was worried about Purvey; and now that so much time had passed, she knew her parents were probably worrying about her too.

Expressing her concerns to Audrey, Lizzie sat down on the steps, folding her arms around herself and began to cry.

"Harvey, run up to Miz Blanton's and ask them to get word to Lizzie's folks at her house. Let them know Lizzie is okay and that the men are looking for Purvey."

Harvey took off running at the first mention of his going anywhere. He was pretty upset as it was. First of all, Henry had let Billy go to Vertie and Bud's, and he had wanted to go too. Then when he and Dempsey asked to go look for Uncle Purvey, Henry had said no again. It was true Dempsey didn't see very well at night, but why couldn't he go? But now he had an important job that only he could do. He was running at top speed with his jacket swinging back and forth behind him as he swung his arms, bent at the elbow, from side to side.

"Lizzie, I sent Harvey to get word to your folks." Audrey wasn't sure Lizzie had heard her, but she didn't repeat herself. She just put more coffee on and told Chris to feed the other children. It might very well be a long night.

After checking on the children and seeing that Chris had everything under control, Audrey grabbed another quilt and sat down on the steps with Lizzie. She put her arm over Lizzie's shoulder pulling the quilt around both of them. They strained to watch the lights bob up and down as the men went farther and farther into the woods. The same woods that had brought them such pleasure in the summer seemed very ominous now.

Audrey could hear Mr. Cagle's hound dogs baying. She had sat with Henry many nights listening to the dogs run the ridge, treeing small animals. She hoped that this time they were looking for Purvey and not a coon. Straining to hear something, she thought she heard one of the men yell, "Over here!" Or had she just imagined it?

Lizzie had finally quit crying, and like Audrey, she was using all her senses, straining to hear and see what was going on back in the woods.

Harvey was back and reported that the Blanton's hired hand, who hadn't been there earlier when they were getting the search party together, had since come home and was on his way to alert the Pruitt family about Purvey and Lizzie.

"Thank you, son, that was a good job. Now go on inside and have Chris fix you a plate. Help her with the little ones. Okay?"

Harvey nodded and went through the back door calling for Dempsey. He, no doubt, wanted to tell him about going up to the Blanton's in the dark, all by himself.

Lizzie stood up putting her hand over her eyes as if shading them from the sun. She was looking towards the woods, not in the same area that the men had started out in, but more to the left where the Washborne boys had built the bridge over the creek.

Nobody used the bridge much anymore. The creek had only recently gotten high enough to make crossing difficult. All during the summer the creek had barely moved. But they had just had an unusually wet October and November.

Audrey decided it was possible Purvey had not been able to cross farther up and had decided to come over the bridge. Maybe the men were just moving down that way because they couldn't get across either. She felt sure Purvey was on this side of the creek, if he was out there at all.

Audrey joined Lizzie on the bottom step and looked in the direction Lizzie was staring. It did look like a lantern was coming closer. Maybe they had found Purvey and had sent someone back to let them know. Audrey prayed she was correct in her assumptions. It was John Cagle.

"They found him. They found him." Lizzie said, as she and Audrey ran towards John.

"Henry sent me back to tell you they found him."

Audrey and Lizzie were both talking at once. "Is he okay? What happened? Where's he been?"

"Whoa, Miss Audrey, Miss Lizzie, slow down some. I don't know, don't know any of those answers. We was just all spread out; and I was the closest one back this way, so they relayed word back to me that they had found him. So, I came on back to let you know. I do know this, he's up by the bridge, and that ol' creek is way over its banks, couldn't have crossed nowheres else." With that, John walked down to the barn and got Henry's mule, leading it behind him as he started back in the woods.

Audrey thought. *Something must have happened to Purvey's mule. Maybe John wants him to be able to ride back.*

She just couldn't get the picture of John leading that mule into the woods out of her mind. It was then that the truth hit her, Purvey was dead. She couldn't tell how she knew. Maybe it was John's not really telling them anything; or maybe it was just the sight of him leading that mule back into the dark woods. She just knew.

Audrey looked at Lizzie to see if the truth had settled in on her yet; but Lizzie was looking at the spot where John had gone back into the woods, and she would not look at Audrey. She kept her head high looking for Purvey to walk out of the woods.

The tears streamed down Audrey's face as she turned around so Lizzie couldn't see her. Now she faced the back of the house, and she could see headlights pulling into the front yard. She hoped with all her heart that it was Mr. and Mrs. Pruitt. Lizzie was going to need her mother.

The back door opened and framed in the light of the house, Audrey saw Marge and Jim Pruitt as they stepped out on the back porch letting their eyes adjust to the darkness, looking for just one thing, their daughter, Lizzie.

Audrey walked towards them pointing back towards Lizzie. As they passed in the yard, Audrey took Jim's hand and told him, "It doesn't look good. Lizzie needs you." With her tears flowing freely now, Audrey walked into the house. The children were all sitting together in a tight little group waiting on some word. Reba was asleep in Christine's arms and Marie was nodding. Charles had long since given up and was on the floor at Christine's feet asleep, still wearing his dirty jeans with the hole in one knee.

"Harvey, Dempsey, please help Chris get the little ones to bed and then come back in here."

Harvey picked up Charles, and Dempsey took Marie by the hand walking with her to bed. Little Miss Curious, Marie, looked back at her momma as if to ask a question. Marie was good at questions. And if you let her get started, she could question for hours. Audrey leaned over and gave her a hug and said, "just go to bed, sweetie, and we will talk in the morning."

Audrey sat down at the table and waited on her three older children to come back. What was she going to tell them? Right then she did not know. She only knew they were good children; tonight had proved that. She had not heard a peep out of them all evening.

It was now close to eleven o'clock. It did not seem possible that she and Lizzie had sat on the back steps so long. It had been hours since the men went into the woods.

Chris came back in the kitchen first, stopping in front of Audrey expectantly. Audrey stood up and put her arms around her. Soon Harvey and Dempsey joined the little circle. They were all holding on to each other.

"Listen, I don't think Uncle Purvey is okay anymore. I'm sure something isn't right. Aunt Lizzie is going to need all of us to be strong for her. You can come outside now and wait with the rest of us. Just put your coats on first."

Now why did she say that? Audrey didn't know. Maybe it was because they had all behaved like adults the past several hours.

Chris decided to wait in the kitchen and keep the coffee hot. She didn't want to know if her Uncle Purvey wasn't okay, but Harvey and Dempsey joined Audrey on the back porch. Dempsey kept his hand on Harvey. He wasn't fond of the dark, his vision being very limited at night.

The lights were coming closer now. From where Audrey was standing, she could see what looked like two lanterns side by side; then a long gap that could possibly be Henry's mule; then two more lanterns; then further back three lanterns in single file.

Lizzie was standing between her parents, but she was standing tall. If she thought for one minute Purvey was not going to be okay, she wasn't showing it.

Then almost quicker then Audrey thought could be possible the lanterns were in the yard. Henry was coming towards her with a sack—a large fertilizer sack. Somehow Audrey knew that bag held the whole purpose of Purvey's visit. Behind Henry the Cagle boys were leading Henry's mule, and on the mule was Purvey's body.

"Oh, Henry, what happened?" Audrey couldn't take her eyes off the bag he was carrying as if somehow that bag held all the answers to her questions.

Henry put his arms around her, for a while not saying anything, just holding her. Trying not to cry, he told her in a soft voice, "Purvey tried to cross the creek on the Washborne Bridge. It looked like it collapsed beneath him. We found him and his mule beneath the bridge. The water had washed him down a little ways closer to shore, or we wouldn't have been able to get to him tonight." Holding her a little tighter he said, "Audrey, I am so sorry, it breaks my heart to tell you. It looks like the fall broke his neck. I know he did not suffer."

Audrey was sobbing. Knowing and being told were two different things. Now that she knew for sure, it was unbearable. Then she remembered Lizzie, "Oh, Henry, where is Lizzie?" They both turned around searching for her.

Lizzie was standing beside Henry's mule with her hand pushing Purvey's hair out of his face. Her mother and father looked powerless to help her.

"Henry, I have to go to her. Please help me."

Henry and Audrey walked over to Lizzie. "Lizzie, honey, let go of him, honey. Let the men get him down." Lizzie stared at Audrey, and to Audrey it looked like she stared through her.

Audrey and Henry weren't prepared for what happened next. Lizzie slipped to the ground. She fainted as quietly as she had stood waiting for Purvey to come back to her; neither Audrey nor Henry could have caught her.

After Lizzie passed out, it seemed to give everyone else the okay to talk and move. Everyone had been standing around not moving or talking, out of respect for Lizzie. Henry picked Lizzie up and carried her into the house laying her gently on the sofa, which was still setting under the window where Chris and Audrey had placed it when Purvey had been coming for a visit.

"Sug, I've got to get back out there and help the fellows. When Lizzie comes to, give her my love."

It was the longest night of Audrey's life, worse than the night of the rape. At least that night she had slept. Tonight there was no sleep. Lizzie was inconsolable.

Her children were asleep in her parent's car, and nobody wanted to be the ones to wake them. It was finally decided someone should take them home and slip them into their own beds, waiting till morning when they all hoped Lizzie would be able to speak to them.

Jim Pruitt decided he should be the someone, the women needed him the least, so he volunteered to take the children home.

Henry and the other men placed Purvey's body in the bed. Audrey would not let them lay him out on the floor. It did not seem fitting. Henry sent for Doctor Stanley; why at this point he did not know, but that, too, seemed the proper thing to do. The doctor would know what they should do next.

Silence settled over the White household. The men who had helped find Purvey quietly went back to their own homes—some to find a drink, others to tell their wives and seek comfort from them. It was the first time many of them had faced death.

Henry could not take the luxury of a drink. He was the only man left, and it was up to him to talk to Doctor Stanley.

"Henry, I'll notify the coroner, and he will be here at first light to pick up Purvey. It looks like an accident pure and simple, and my report will state that. Wish I could be of more help." Doctor Stanley's visit was short and to the point.

Now looking back, Audrey wondered where that night went. It seemed to pass quickly, but then with seven children to look after, life went on quickly.

Lizzie had finally gone home before the coroner came. She wanted to be there when the children woke up. Although death had come to Audrey's only brother, she couldn't take time to grieve. She knew what lay ahead. Neither she nor Henry had slept at all, but launched right into a full day of activities.

Lizzie pulled herself together and planned Purvey's funeral. She had him brought back home and held a vigil for him. She kept the candles lit all night, and the next morning asked the Cagle boys to hitch up their wagon and place Purvey in the back. It seemed to help her knowing the men who had brought Purvey back to her were there to help her get him to his gravesite.

The little funeral procession made its way down the road. Lizzie and Audrey walked hand in hand behind the wagon. It was a little over two miles to Mount Carmel Church, but they refused to ride. They were like sisters; they both loved Purvey.

From the very first when Purvey married Lizzie, Audrey had been a part of their life. Behind the two women, Henry and Wesley walked, surrounded by the White and Dickinson children. Henry had insisted that Chris and the younger children ride with Bud and Vertie, but the boys walked beside their father.

The mules plodded slowly down the dirt road, and with each step, Audrey and Lizzie let go of Purvey, remembering all the good and bad times they had shared together.

As the slow moving procession continued down the old country road, neighbors stood in their yards and watched. Some joined the family as they walked behind the wagon carrying Purvey's body. By the time they reached the church, there were close to fifty people walking or in cars behind those who had chosen to walk.

Purvey Dickinson was laid to rest near Renee in Mount Carmel's small cemetery, just four days before Reba turned two. It was December 1943, and the sky was clear, a beautiful day in anyone's book.

To Audrey it did not seem right to bury Purvey near Renee, but it was Lizzie's decision. She told Audrey later that Purvey had never gotten over Renee's death, and she wanted him close by so he could finally resolve with Renee what had happened. Audrey knew it had been one of the hardest things she would ever have to do; letting her best friend, her brother, go to his final resting-place.

Lizzie stayed in Double Springs until after Christmas then moved to Culman, Alabama to live with her parents. The day she left, Audrey helped her finish packing. They had loaded the last of the boxes in the back of a truck when Lizzie turned to Audrey and handed her one of Purvey's handkerchiefs.

"Audrey, you probably won't remember, but you gave Purvey this handkerchief when he went to the reform school. See in the corner where you embroidered P.D.? He cherished this hanky and would not use it, but he carried it on Sunday morning without fail to church. I know he wanted you to have it."

Audrey took the hanky, wiping the tears from Lizzie's eyes, then her own. She would never wash those tears out of the handkerchief; they would dry there in remembrance of Purvey, her beloved brother.

Being small has a few
advantages. I'm just not sure
what they are.

—Olivet Dickinson

CHAPTER TWENTY-ONE

"Momma, Momma, I got you a letter!" Charles never said anything quietly when he could yell. He was running as fast as his small legs would allow delivering the letter. A big responsibility, or so Charles thought.

Audrey loved writing letters and receiving letters, so each one was like a Christmas present to her, an unknown gift from some special place. Sure enough it was a letter, and it was from Olivet. He had promised to write her when he joined the Navy, and now she had her first letter from him since he left almost six months ago.

Audrey placed Reba down gently on a quilt and settled herself down in her rocker on the porch. She took a last look around, locating all the children: Marie was playing with her dolls; Charles was trying to get Dempsey and Harvey to let him join their marble game; Christine was in the house somewhere. Satisfied that she was aware of what was going on, she opened her letter, enjoying each word she read.

Dear Audrey, Henry, and children,

I miss you all. It's not so bad here. How's the children? Wish I could see you all.

I like my Navy uniform. The fellows here are all farmers, like me, so we look out for each other.

Momma said in her last letter that you and Henry were expecting another little one. I wish you the best. Is this number eight?

She wrote that Ruth and Aileen (they were his younger sisters) were seeing those Elenburg boys, Leldon and Leon. It's a-worrying her some. Ammon and Joe are a doing okay, I guess. Jack's in another camp, not close to me though.

Did get to see him a few weeks back. I was going into town or a-trying too, when a bus plumb full of sailors comes by. They said there was always room for one more, so I climbed through a window, what with some fellows pushing me up and the others pulling me in. I looked up to see the one pulling me in, and it was Jack. It was so good to see him!

His troop was being transported to another camp. We had a short visit. Too short. Before I knew it, I was going out the way I come in.

Jack sends his best.

We got to laughing and reminiscing 'bout the time I broke his nose. Being shorter than most folks worked for me on my trip to town, and getting to see Jack and all, I guess I'm more used to it now. Could have saved poor ol' Jack's nose or Momma's cornbread one, if I had been used to it back then. (Olivet was the smallest, and one day Jack had been teasing him unbearably, or so Olivet thought at the time. He grabbed a piece of Aunt Viola's cornbread from the night before and hit Jack just right breaking his nose. From then on they quit teasing him, but the family always had to tell that tale on Olivet.)

Audrey had another laugh after reading about the incident again. Olivet was about 5'2" and the rest of the family was head and shoulders taller than he was, including the girls. Audrey would have to find out what was going on with the said girls. Dating were they? Maybe a wedding in the Dickinson family would be coming up soon.

Going back to her letter, Audrey's eyes misted over while reading the next part of Olivet's letter.

Momma's eyes seem to be getting worse. She's suffering with them bad headaches again. (Viola had horrible headaches that would put her to bed for a day or two at a time. Audrey was very sorry that they were still happening.)

Well, Audrey I'll close. Good luck on the new baby. Pat Henry on the back for me.

Belzie Blanton has been writing me some; maybe we will get together when I get home.

Your loving cousin,
Olivet

Audrey smiled thinking of Belzie and Olivet as a couple. Belzie was about 4'10"—just the right size for Olivet. They would be a sight to see.

She folded the letter back up planning to read it to Henry over supper. Thinking of that, she rocked slowly and planned dinner in between thoughts of the letter. *I'll write him back, after we put the children to bed.*

Bad things happen sometimes.
Don't mean it's God's doin',
don't mean it's not.

—Wesley Dickinson

CHAPTER TWENTY-TWO

Enjoying the peace and quiet, Audrey was in deep thought, as she leisurely swept the yard. The sand was hard, packed from so much activity. She or Christine swept it clean every morning, just a daily chore—no grass or weeds were allowed in this yard.

Looking up for no particular reason, she saw Christine and Reba coming towards her; and the two other children were running behind Christine, a bucket bouncing around between them. They had been down in the lower pasture—Marie, Charles, Reba, and Christine—picking blackberries. She wasn't expecting them back quite so soon. The way they were running, if they had picked any blackberries, they were probably on the ground. The bucket was bouncing every which way.

The first thing Audrey saw was the blood. It was the brightest color she had ever seen, an almost pink red. She couldn't be sure if it was coming from Christine or Reba, since Christine had three-year-old Reba in her arms. Christine, who appeared to be running as fast as she could, was every now and then looking over her shoulder, encouraging the other two to hurry up.

Christine began yelling. As she got closer Audrey was able to make out what she was saying. "Momma, Reba fell playing around on the glade rocks; her nose is bleeding, and it won't stop!"

Audrey let Christine hand her Reba as she slid into a chair on the porch. "Chris get a towel and cold water from the well. Hurry!"

Audrey tried everything: holding Reba's head back, which caused her to choke, applying pressure on her nose while one towel after another was soaked with blood. It was spurting everywhere.

The mailman, Mr. Morton, was up on the main road near the mailbox. He was used to one or two of the White children racing up for the mail, so he stopped to wait.

Audrey, looking up, noticed him sitting up there and motioned to Christine. "Go get Mr. Morton, Reba's got to go to the doctor."

Shuffling through the mail one more time, Mr. Morton seemed some what surprised to see Christine coming for the mail.

"Mr. Morton, Mr. Morton, Reba's hurt, Momma wants to know if you'll take her to the doctor?"

"Well sure, this mail will wait. What seems to be the problem?" He talked as he maneuvered the car into the yard, driving slowly so Chris could keep up. She was walking beside the car telling him what happened.

Charles and Marie had finally caught up with Chris and were standing there with juice from the blackberries covering their faces. They were still holding on to the bucket.

After a quick discussion, it was decided Christine would go with Reba. Audrey, being over eight months pregnant, and by now covered with Reba's blood, thought she best stay right where she was. She trusted Christine to look after Reba as well as she could.

Christine changed her blouse, and with two towels and a blanket, even though it had to be in the 80s, they were ready.

Reba wasn't crying anymore, but she was white as a sheet and appeared even whiter with the bright blood all over her.

Mr. Morton headed straight for Dr. Stanley's office, never slowing down—not even for Miss Wilson who was waving a letter at him she wanted to mail.

"Well, I never," Miss Wilson muttered as she stomped back up to her house.

"I'm sorry Mr. Morton, I bet Miss Wilson will be mad at you."

"Not to worry Miss Christine, she'll get over it. I'll soothe her feelings later. Actually she is one of my favorites, always bringing me a sample of her latest cake or pie and sometimes a large glass of fresh lemonade or tea, a really nice lady. But I'm sure she will understand when I tell her about Reba, and this little emergency."

Dr. Stanley's office was full, but his wife Jane, who was there trying to help out for the day, took Chris by the arm and moved her and Reba through a door to the back of the office. Moments later she had the doctor there.

He had walked out and left Suzy Barton, who had just started on her third ailment that she needed to discuss with him.

"Well, Miss Christine what have we here?" Doctor Stanley knew the White children all by name. He was there at the majority of the children's birth.

"It's Reba. She hit her nose, and it won't quit bleeding. Momma tried everything then Mr. Morton brought us here."

"Okay, let's have a look. Jane, get Mr. Morton on his way. We'll get Christine and Reba home some other way."

Jane was going through the door when the doctor said, "Oh, yeah, send Sally Ann in here to assist me, and take a minute to speak to Suzy Barton."

Sally Ann Hasket had been Doctor Stanley's assistant as long as he could remember. She was good at handling patients, especially little ones. Jane was better at soothing the often-cranky older ones, who seemed more like children every day.

First he tried packing Reba's nose with gauze, and that didn't last long. As he worked, trying first one thing then another, he kept up a running conversation with Christine. "How's your Momma? Bout time for the new baby?"

Chris was hovering over Reba and had to be moved aside once or twice by Dr. Stanley or Sally Ann. Answering the doctor's question with a simple yes or no, she scooted up for another look. This time a sleeping Reba holding on to a bright red lollipop rewarded her for her trouble. Christine noticed the blood had finally stopped. Reba appeared quite peaceful now.

Dr. Stanley had to cauterize the interior of her nose, as he explained to Christine. Reba had managed to bust every little blood vessel in there, and her little body wasn't healing fast enough to stop the bleeding. So he helped it along. Reba still had gauze in her nose, but he said in an hour or two they could pull it out.

"Christine, honey, just get comfortable. The doctor wants to watch Reba awhile then we will drive you home. He has to sift through a few more patients, besides Miss Audrey just might need a look-see herself, or so the doctor said." Personally, Jane thought he wanted to keep an eye on Reba just a little longer, but she did not relay that information to Christine. Poor girl was worried enough as it was.

It was a little longer than two hours, but true to his word, Dr. Stanley took the girls home. Jane tagged along so she could hold Reba a little longer. She was such a sweet, loving child, bright green eyes and blonde, almost white, hair.

Audrey had walked the floor for what seemed to her like days. Mr. Morton had stopped back by to report they had gotten to the doctor and to relay the message Doctor Stanley had sent about bringing the girls home. "They will be fine," he assured her.

Finally they were pulling into the yard—Christine in the back of Dr. Stanley's car with Reba sitting on Jane's lap in the front.

"Good afternoon, Miss Audrey. You've had quite a day, I imagine. She's fine. Yes, I'm sure. Kept her a while to be sure. These things happen some times. Just keep a close eye on her for a day or two. Shouldn't happen again, but if it does, get her to me as fast as you can."

"Jane, you can put Miss Reba down now. You're a big girl aren't you Reba?"

"Now, Audrey, what's your news?"

The other children were all vying for Reba's attention, but she was still holding on to Jane's hand while holding her lollipop with her other hand and not looking like she was in any hurry to move.

"Any pains? Think you'll need me this time?"

Audrey laughed, "No, I think Suz and I will be okay. She's checking almost daily now for signs. I'll have Henry come by and settle up for today; he hasn't come in from work yet."

"Thank you, Doctor Stanley, and you too, Jane. You always seem to be helping me out of messes. I was pretty scared. She seemed so pale and there was so much blood."

Reba was okay, but she never did get her rosy coloring back, she was always very pale. And she refused to go berry picking and had no liking for blackberries. Even blackberry pie did not tempt Reba.

Sometimes the past is more
real than the present
or the future.

—Audrey Dickinson

CHAPTER TWENTY-THREE

When Audrey finally told Henry about the new baby, they agreed if it was a boy that they would name him after Purvey.

She measured time now by how many months it had been since Purvey died. She couldn't seem to focus on the future; the past loomed way too large. She insisted on visiting Purvey's grave every Sunday after church.

Sometimes Henry and the children would walk over to the cemetery with her, but more often than not, she went alone. Audrey told Purvey all that was going on in her little family, what each child had done the week before and when the new baby was due, which was very soon.

On the Fourth of July she asked Henry to drive her over to the church. He parked as close to the cemetery as he could get so she would not have so far to walk. She was large with this baby who, according to Suz, was late and should have been born the week before.

Audrey wanted one last visit with Purvey before she was confined with the new baby. The day looked almost like the twin of the day they had buried Purvey. It was hotter, but the same clear sky was overhead, with beautiful, white, billowing clouds floating past.

"Purvey, it has been seven months since you left; and I still miss you. Henry and the children help, but it was always me and you against the world." Audrey cried and knelt down patting the grave with her right hand as she wiped the tears from her eyes with her left.

As she sat there, the peace she had sought seemed to pour into her body from all sides. At last she thought, *Purvey, I can finally let you go.*

The child moving inside of her below her heart seemed to feel this new found peace also and lay still, not moving but quietly waiting.

"Henry, will you come help me up?" Audrey was looking around trying to find Henry. He usually walked away while she and Purvey talked. She called a little louder, "Henry!"

Henry was strolling through the cemetery looking at all the names on the tombstones. Some he knew, because he had been there when they were buried; others he was just curious about. Some of the dates were over fifty years old, and some of the newer ones were babies buried within days of their birth. He thanked God for his boys and girls who were healthy. "And while I'm at it, God, thank you for our new baby too; and, God, can you make it soon. I know Audrey is ready, and I have been ready a long time now." It was then that he heard Audrey calling him. "That was fast, Lord."

Audrey wasn't in labor. She had just gotten down and could not balance herself to get back up. By the time Henry got to her, she was laughing hysterically.

"Oh, Henry, look at me. I'm a mess. I can't get up from here, and if I didn't know better, I would think Purvey is laughing at me too." Henry helped Audrey get up, and they drove home in silence, but for once it seemed to be a comfortable silence.

Audrey appeared different to him, quieter and at peace with herself. He could still hear her laughter. It was so good to hear her laugh. He hoped with all his heart she would laugh more often now.

Purvey's death had been hard on them all. Audrey especially felt guilty because he had been on his way to see her. The peanuts he was bringing her were still in the bag; she could not bring herself to eat them.

Two days after Audrey's visit to the cemetery, Cecilia Faye White made her way into the world. Considering all the stress Audrey had endured the past year, Faye's birth was one of the easiest.

Audrey thought it must have been all the ice cream she had eaten on the Fourth of July that had caused Faye to come so easily two days later, or maybe it was the new peace she had with herself.

Even Suz said, "Audrey, you didn't need me or the doctor on this one."

Since Faye was born on the anniversary of Selah's death, Audrey named her for Selah, or Sealey as she had been called. Thus the name Cecilia, but Audrey determined she would call her Faye.

Every Fourth of July Henry and the boys went to the icehouse and brought back enough ice to make homemade ice cream. This year they had made two different kinds, first vanilla and then strawberry. Audrey mixed two jars of strawberry jam into her recipe for vanilla, and Henry turned the handle on the old ice cream churn until the smell of fresh strawberries filled the air. Thinking about it now, Audrey could eat another dish full.

Well, maybe not, Faye was crying; she wanted her dinner. This new child with the dark black hair and dark eyes looked so much like Henry, with his dark hair and dark eyes. All the other children had taken after the Dickinson family, fair of skin and hair. They had a house full of white-headed young'uns, now this little Indian maiden. For, in truth, that is what she looked like, a little Indian child with a ready-made tan. Audrey wondered if Paralee would find it so easy to ignore this one. She thought not, as Paralee set great store by their Indian heritage.

* * * * *

Henry took the older children and went to see Paralee and Will. His mission was to tell them all about Faye and to invite them for a visit. Audrey was feeling like her old self. Now, she was ready to get up and see a few people. Chris, at almost thirteen, could keep house and cook as well as Audrey, so he knew that with Christine's help it would not be too much for Audrey.

Henry wanted his parents to come spend the day. Basically Henry was very family oriented and checked on his parents often. He and his brothers rarely missed a week seeing each other.

"Will, get out here. Henry and the children are a-coming." Paralee was sitting on the front porch dipping snuff, periodically spitting into her spit can. She had a sweet gum toothbrush in her right hand and began to methodically brush her teeth. The snuff turned her teeth a brownish color, so every now and then; she would rinse her mouth out with water and then brush her teeth up and down with the little brush from a sweet gum tree that grew in their yard.

Will had gone into the kitchen to get himself a snack; but at the first mention of Henry and the children, he decided the snack could wait.

"Now, I wonder what has brought that boy over here in the middle of the week." Paralee was being her usual self; not much went unnoticed by her.

Henry normally worked every day but Sunday, so for him to be here in the middle of the week seemed strange to her.

"Hey, Daddy, hey, Momma, good to see you. Bet Daddy was in the house looking for something good to eat. Charles was yelling all the way down the road that he could see Grandma but not Granddaddy." Henry knew his father very well. Will always made himself a snack, which was usually about thirty minutes after his midday meal. Paralee cooked a large breakfast and dinner, but they often had a light supper. So Will always snacked in between.

"Henry, what are you doing here in the middle of the week? Where's that boy Billy, and Christine?" Paralee rarely asked about Audrey, but Henry never let it bother him.

"Slow down, Momma, one question at a time. I'm on the night shift at the mine this week, don't have to be there till 'bout four. Bill White is working with the Cagles this week. They're doing some logging. Chris is helping her momma."

Charles had climbed up in Will's lap, and Dempsey was trying to catch Marie. The minute their feet touched the ground, they were off and running. Reba walked over to Paralee, not saying anything but standing within arms reach. Harvey nodded at his grandparents and headed for the rear of the house where Will kept his huntin' dogs.

Paralee absent-mindedly patted Reba on the head but didn't offer to pick her up or give her a hug. Reba was a very loving child, and since Paralee wasn't acting like she wanted to hold her, she walked over and crawled up in her daddy's lap.

As always, Will let Paralee do all the talking. He was busy tickling Charles and pretending to pull pennies out of his ears.

"Are you hungry, Henry, you or the children?"

"No, ma'am, we had dinner before we left home."

"When you going to tell her, Daddy?" Reba was looking up at Henry with a quizzical look on her little face.

"You tell her, pumpkin. Grandma would probably rather hear the news from you than me."

"What news is that?" Actually Paralee knew Audrey was expecting again, so after a few minutes she figured that was what this visit was all about. *Probably had the baby, at least we know this one is Henry's*, Paralee had never forgiven Audrey for Billy Hugh or Chris who she still didn't think belonged to Henry.

"Grandma, we got a baby. Her name is Faye."

"You don't say." Paralee spoke to Reba but was looking at Henry.

"When did Faye make her appearance?"

Will quit tickling Charles long enough to ask, "Yeah, son, when did the new little one get here?"

"On the sixth, Daddy. Audrey named her after her mother Selah. Her name is Cecilia Faye. She was born on the anniversary of Selah's death."

"Well, congratulations, son. Another little girl. Now Miss Reba will have a playmate. These ol' boys play too rough, don't they little gal?" As he questioned her, Will leaned over and poked his finger at her, causing Reba to giggle and snuggle up closer to her daddy.

"Actually we came by to ask you to come to dinner on Sunday and see your latest granddaughter. Vertie and Bud and their children will be there too."

"Of course, son, we'll be there. Won't we Paralee?"

"I think, Momma, this one is going to surprise you. She's quite the beauty, isn't she Reba?"

Reba only nodded, for Marie and Dempsey playing in the yard had distracted her. Turning around backwards, she climbed down from Henry's lap and scooted down the steps on her bottom. Landing with a thud on the last step, she jumped up and took off after Marie.

Paralee agreed that they would be there Sunday about noon.

Henry gathered up his brood and, waving bye to his parents, started down the road headed for home. This was the only place he ever took his children that one or more did not beg to stay.

"Wonder why?" he asked himself out loud. He knew they all loved Will. "It must be Momma. Maybe they are afraid of her." Henry had guessed correctly. They all loved Will, but Paralee intimidated them all. Henry was so used to her ways that he never noticed until today.

Today he noticed the look on Reba's face, for she was rarely turned down when it came to affection. True Paralee had not been overly affectionate, but Will had always made up for it, hugging the boys and girls alike.

Will and Paralee did come to dinner, and Audrey was right. Paralee took one look at Faye and picked her up. Henry could not remember her holding any of the others. Maybe she had, but looking at Audrey over his mother's head, he knew his first memory was the correct one. Even Will was looking at Paralee strangely. She was holding one of Audrey's children.

Audrey patted Will on the shoulder, not saying anything, just letting him know she was there. Telling him without words that she was glad they came.

That day was one to remember in the White house, for Paralee had not only held Faye, but also changed and rocked her too. She would have fed her no doubt, but Audrey was nursing this one as she had all the others.

Every marriage
has a beginning and an ending.
It's what's in the middle that counts.

—Abraham Dickinson

CHAPTER TWENTY-FOUR

"Henry, do you mean it? Can we really go meet Olivet's bus?"

"Sure, Sug, I don't know why not."

Audrey's favorite cousin Olivet was coming home from the Navy. His bus was scheduled to arrive the next afternoon in Haleyville.

Viola and Abraham had been at church on Sunday. The preacher at Mount Carmel had asked Abraham to conduct a revival at his church. Abraham Dickinson, being well known in Double Springs, Alabama, had often preached as a visiting preacher. Several years back they had moved to Lynn, Alabama, where Abraham pastored a church. So it was not unusual for them to be in the area, but this was the first time they had stayed with Henry, Audrey, and the children. They stayed two days before going back to their home church.

It was during that visit that Viola had told Audrey that Olivet was coming home. The war was over, and Olivet's tour with the Navy was up. He had never left the states and had been so homesick he did not want to re-enlist. Olivet was twenty-seven, and Viola was hoping he would settle down and get married. She wanted more grandchildren.

Since Purvey's death, Audrey had written Olivet often, and in some respects, Olivet had taken Purveys place in Audrey's heart. So she was very excited about Olivet's homecoming, and Henry had just said they would go meet the bus.

Audrey knew Olivet had also been writing to Belzie. She wondered if Belzie knew he was coming home.

"Maybe I'll walk up to the Blanton's and visit for awhile. It would be nice to see Evie and Belzie; maybe Shelly's husband is coming home too. You don't mind do you Henry?"

"No, go ahead, I'm gonna go down to the barn and see what needs to be done to fix Mac's stall. The boys said he busted out again."

"I'll take Faye with me, if you'll keep one ear tuned to what Charles is up to."

Shelly, Belzie's sister, was married to one of the Curtis boys, Lowell, who was in the Army. He had been stationed in Colorado. Evie and Belzie had surprised everyone by going out there for three months to be with Shelly who had recently given birth to a little boy. Terry, she thought they had named him.

They had only been home a few weeks, but Audrey had not seen them. Getting her sunbonnet and leaving Chris in charge, she took Faye and walked up the hill to the Blanton home place. It was a beautiful, fall day; all the trees were turning the most beautiful reds and golds. Every year Audrey did not think it could get any prettier, but every year it did, or so it seemed.

Belzie and Evie were sitting on the front porch of the large Blanton home place. Whit had built a porch that almost encircled the whole house. It was on three sides with several doors going into the main house from the porch areas. The driveway circled behind the house with two exits to the main road. Belzie and Evie were sitting on the porch facing the road and began waving at Audrey as she came up the road.

Whit had been dead for some years now, but his presence was still felt in the Blanton family. He had been a hard man, ruling his family with an iron fist. A strong man of God who traveled between two churches preaching, often getting paid in syrup or vegetables.

He ran a large farm, hiring local boys, blacks and whites. Whit had hired a black nanny for one of his boys when his first wife Hannah's milk had run out. He was not a prejudiced man as a lot of his age group were. Criticized by many, his only counsel was God.

Whit left his large estate to Belzie and Hardy with provisions for Evie to be cared for. Whit had twelve children, but Hardy and Belzie were the only two children at home, so it was felt he was providing for the two children living under his roof. A road going into Double Springs divided the division of the property line. Belzie was given the side with the house and Hardy the side with the barn. The will was simply stated. There were no maps or drawings of property lines, just the road saying one side was Belzie's and one side Hardy's. He had previously given Belzie twelve acres to build a home on when she got married. The same offer had been given to all his children, with some choosing money rather than land.

Whit would name his twelve children to anyone who would listen making a rhyme of it. Taylor, Eva, Bob and Paul, Ada, May and Ray,

Ora, Nora, Hardy, Belzie, and Shelly Faye. The first eight belonged to Hannah, who died when Ora was about two. Evie raised his eight and had four more.

Belzie was very talented. She could draw and paint most anything; today she was putting the finishing touches on some pottery she had been working on. She would take the Alabama clay and fashion it into animals, mostly cats and dogs as the Blanton's had a plentiful supply of both that could be used as models. Then she would set them in the hot Alabama sun, letting them dry completely. After that she would paint the various pieces she had completed, often selling one or more pieces to visitors in the area.

"Hello, Audrey, come set a spell with us." Evie loved company. "We are just letting our lunch settle. At least I am. Belzie can't be still, so she is painting on a dog this time."

"Hello, Evie, Belzie. It sure is a beautiful day, don't you think?" As she spoke, Audrey sat down in the rocker Evie offered.

"It sure is," Belzie was wiping her hands off in preparation of picking up Faye. Belzie loved children, and she was a big favorite of her nieces and nephews. Her sisters and brothers considered Belzie, at thirty-two a spinster. She was very small, barely 4'10", so all the children just thought she was one of them since she had a playful spirit, always ready for a game. Evie's grandchildren did not come to see her, but wanted to come play with Aunt Belzie.

* * * * *

When Whit was still alive, Belzie had dated some and had fallen in love with John Dinsmore. Whit did not approve, but Belzie had been determined to have her way. She heard all the gossips talk about him and his wild ways, but Belzie was in love.

Whit finally forbade her to see him, but Hardy couldn't resist Belzie's plea for his aid in seeing John. So he would take his girl and double date with Belzie. Thinking Hardy would watch out for Belzie, Whit would let her go. They would just fail to tell Whit who Belzie's date was going to be. Whit caught on to what was going on and decided to prove to Belzie what type of person John Dinsmore was. Whit had heard John was also seeing the Taylor girl on the side. So, seeking to prove this to Belzie, he asked her to ride over to the Taylor place with him.

Belzie, thinking someone was sick and needed prayer, went willingly enough with him. Evie decided at the last minute that she would go too.

Right before getting to the Taylor homestead there was an old rundown house that had seen better days. When Whit pulled in there, Belzie was really puzzled. What were they doing at an empty house? There were quilts covering the windows, and it looked empty to her. Whit knew better. He had heard that John Dinsmore and Wanda Taylor had been staying there quite openly, and he had decided the only way to make Belzie see him for the type of man he knew him to be was to simply show her.

As they came to a stop, John came out the front door and right behind him, about half-dressed, stood Wanda. Seeing Belzie, John tried to grab the reins of the horse to keep Whit from leaving till he could talk to Belzie.

Evie, almost the same size as Belzie, grabbed the whip from the small stand that Whit kept it in and, standing up in the wagon, lashed out at John before Whit could stop her. Belzie, in shock, was crying softly. The fact that John was exactly the kind of man her father had been telling her was upsetting enough, but she had never seen her mother raise her voice or hand to man or animal; and evidently neither had her father.

Whit leaned over, taking the whip from Evie. He said very calmly, "Sit down Evie, we're going home now."

The subject of John Dinsmore never came up after that day. Evie didn't mention it to Belzie and neither did Whit, but Belzie never forgave her father for being right and loved her mother all the more. After that she did not date for a long time.

When Shelly began dating Lowell, Belzie started dating another Curtis boy, but, again Whit intervened, saying he was too large a man for Belzie. Fats, as he was called, was tall and heavyset. This time Belzie did not fight him but simply quit dating altogether. She felt like Whit was never going to be happy with anyone she chose.

* * * * *

Belzie grew up knowing Olivet, and since her brother Hardy and several of his friends were in the service, she wrote to them all. So

Audrey didn't know if Belzie was interested in Olivet as a man or just as one of her many friends.

"Olivet is coming home. Aunt Viola told me on Sunday that he would be here next Saturday. He is coming in on the bus to Haleyville." Audrey watched Belzie closely as she told the two of them her news.

"Oh, I have always liked Olivet," Evie said. "I'm glad he is coming home. So many of our boys aren't. Hardy has another year to serve, and Lowell has decided to stay another term."

Belzie continued to play with Faye and didn't seem to be paying too much attention to her mother and Audrey. But Audrey had seen a little flicker in her eyes and a blush in her cheeks. Maybe Belzie was just a little bit interested.

"Did Belzie tell you about our trip to Colorado?" Evie kept on talking.

"No ma'am, I knew you went, but I haven't heard about it. Did you have a good time?"

"Yes, it was beautiful, Shelly had the baby while we were there, and Belzie worked in a fish hook factory."

Audrey wanted to laugh but thought better of it. "A fish hook factory?"

"Yes, they made fish hooks, and Belzie brought home several for her scrap book. She didn't work long, but it helped keep her busy."

"Did you like working Belzie?" Audrey still trying not to laugh about fish hooks looked at Belzie expectantly.

"It was okay. Like Momma said, I didn't work too long. The truth is we were both so homesick, that after Terry was born, we decided to come back home. Shelly and Lowell stayed, but he is to be transferred back this way soon. Maybe over in Georgia." That was the most Belzie had spoken since Audrey had walked up.

"Henry said we could drive up to Haleyville and see Olivet when he gets here. Thought we might take Faye, since he has never seen her. Would you and Evie like to go?"

"Oh, Audrey, that is so sweet of you to ask us, but I better not, Belzie might want to."

They both turned and looked at Belzie looking for an answer.

Taking a few more minutes, Belzie nodded her head yes. "That is if you don't need me for anything, Momma."

"Of course not. You go ahead and give Olivet my love. Invite that boy to dinner too." Evie reached for Faye. She obviously thought

Belzie's turn holding the little one had lasted long enough.

Belzie went into the house. getting them all a glass of iced tea. Stepping back on the porch with a tray with the tea and some cookies on it, she asked Audrey, "What time will we be leaving?"

"About ten, I think. If I remember right, Aunt Viola said the bus would be in about noon. I'll have Henry ask at the bus station in town what time the bus in Haleyville is due, to be sure." Audrey answered Belzie's question as she nibbled on a cookie.

"These cookies are really good. Did you make them Belzie?" Audrey had been trying to draw Belzie into the conversation ever since she had walked up and sat down. Belzie only nodded and went back to her painting, so Audrey decided to talk to Evie a little more before she went home.

"Have you heard anything from Nora lately? I haven't seen her since she and Leonard McCrary got married."

"Oh, she's fine. They have a little boy now and another baby on the way. Leonard is farming, and they are doing okay. It's about time for them to scoot over for a visit. I'll tell her to stop by and see you."

"Well, I guess Faye and I better get home before Christine thinks I have run off and left her. She would never forgive me if she had to raise Charles. He is such a handful, all boy."

Audrey set her glass down and picked up Faye, who looked like she could use a nap after all the excitement and attention.

"Audrey, why don't I walk part way home with you? Momma I'll be back in a few minutes." Belzie stuck her paintbrushes in a glass of turpentine and wiped her hands off, offering to carry Faye for Audrey.

"Audrey, be sure and come see us again, and bring Reba and Marie too. I'm sure they have both grown a lot since we last saw them." Evie picked up the glasses and started toward the kitchen as she bid Audrey good bye.

They had only taken a few steps when Belzie started talking. "I've been writing to Olivet quite a bit. I usually let Momma read his letters too, only this last one I haven't showed anyone. Audrey, he said he loved me. We wrote while I was in Colorado, too, and mostly we just wrote about stuff happening in the area and family and such; so when he said he loved me, I didn't know what he really meant or how I felt."

Audrey looked at Belzie with a surprised look, not that she was surprised that Olivet had told her he loved her, but more a wondering of what effect Olivet's declaration had on Belzie. But other than showing interest in the conversation, Audrey did little talking. She just listened intently to Belzie and her reasoning where Olivet was concerned.

"Momma likes him, and if Daddy were alive, I'm sure he would say he is just the right size. We're probably the smallest people in Winston County." So in that respect they did seem to be fitted to each other. But Audrey thought that was no reason for a marriage if that was what all this was leading up to.

"Anyway, I would like very much to go meet his bus with you. I haven't seen Olivet in over a year." Handing Faye back to Audrey, Belzie turned and started home.

Audrey just shook her head; she was more confused then ever.

* * * * *

"Momma, relax. We will be just fine." Chris was trying to help her mother and father get on their way.

Audrey often left Chris in charge for short trips up the road to a neighbor's house, or to go to the doctor. She and Henry rarely left at the same time and not for long periods of time.

Today they would be gone for five or six hours. First the drive to Haleyville to meet Olivet, then they would visit for awhile, have dinner and drive home.

As Chris was still trying to pack a bag with all the things Faye would need, inching her mother toward the door, Belzie walked into the yard.

"Momma, Miss Blanton is here." You could hear Charles' voice above the din of barking dogs and children running across the porch and jumping into the yard, the latest game one of them had come up with.

"Belzie, we would have stopped by and picked you up. You didn't have to walk all the way down here." Audrey picked up Faye and walked on out on the porch looking over her shoulder for Henry as she did.

"That's okay, I needed a breath of fresh air." Belzie stooped down and shook hands with Charles and put her arm on Marie's shoulder, walking up to Audrey.

"Charles, where is your daddy?" Charles had just charged past her on another trip across the porch, jumping off the end over a bush.

Breathing hard, Charles replied, "In the barn." Landing on his feet, he was up and running for another go round when Audrey stuck her hand out and stopped him.

"Go get your Daddy. We are ready."

Spinning around on one foot, he headed toward the barn as if that had been his true destination. "Daddy, Daddy, Momma wants you."

"I could have done that," Audrey thought out loud. "Come on Belzie; we will get in the truck. Chris, don't forget what I said, keep an eye on these children, and if you have any problems, Miss Cagle and Mrs. Blanton are home."

"Yes, Momma, I know." Chris was tired of hearing the same instructions over and over again. She wished they would just go on.

Henry was walking across the yard with Charles two steps behind him, trying to stretch his small legs into big steps like his daddy. Henry stopped and turned around quickly catching Charles by surprise, and Charles ran right into his daddy's arms. Henry swung him up in the air and put him down on the porch. "Boy you better be good for Chris, or when I get home—" Henry never finished his threat and Charles was off and running again.

Henry patted Reba and Marie on their heads and climbed up in the truck with Audrey and Belzie, who was holding Faye. "Everybody ready? Got everything you need, Sug?"

"Yes, Henry, we're ready. Don't forget, Chris, keep a eye on these children—especially Charles." Henry was halfway out of the yard, and Audrey was still yelling instructions to Christine.

"She'll do fine, Audrey. Just set back and enjoy the ride."

If Audrey had any doubts about the way Belzie and Olivet felt about each other, they were set aside by the end of that visit. For there was no doubt that there was a spark of something going on, as they had barely taken their eyes off of each other all afternoon. When it was time to leave and start back home, Olivet hugged and kissed Belzie, before helping her back into Henry's truck for their trip home. From where Audrey was sitting it looked like a mutual kiss that was quite intense.

"See you Sunday," Olivet said.

As far as Audrey knew, that was the way it officially started, Belzie and Olivet and Sundays at this church or that. "Courtin'," as the country folk called it.

Just as I was. That was the way
Henry took me, and I don't
think he has ever been sorry.
I know I haven't.

—Audrey Dickinson

CHAPTER TWENTY-FIVE

Audrey gazed longingly out the kitchen window, but all she saw was the wash house beckoning her. Henry had built it for her last year. He had said laundry was hard enough with so many young'uns, the least he could do was build her a wash house.

It was an old, wood building with a tin roof about 12' x 12', a door and two windows with wooden coverings that could be bolted up in the summer or shut down tight in the winter. There was a wood stove to heat water to wash with, and in the summertime she could do her canning out there, keeping the heat out of the house. The wash house doubled as a bathhouse. Audrey made sure the children bathed daily, but those were normally just sponge baths; so on Saturday it was an all over bath in the wash house, summer and winter.

It definitely was wash day. Henry's overalls were all dirty, everything was dirty! She already had Christine changing the beds, just the way she had taught her. Take the top sheet and make it the bottom sheet and put a clean top sheet on. They were only fertilizer sacks sewed together for sheets, but they were all they had; and they were always clean.

Audrey knew she needed to get started, but this new baby seemed to sap her energy. Maybe another cup of coffee, and then she could get it together.

Harvey was dragging out the big wash pot, and Dempsey was starting the fire. Marie and Charles were pouring buckets of water into the pot from the well, getting almost as much water on themselves as in the pot.

Audrey loved each and every one of those precious children. They were good young'uns, as Henry was prone to call them.

A swift kick in her side reminded her of the new life. It was as if he or she were saying, "What about me?"

That was it. She decided it was time she joined them out there. But tomorrow she was going to have a holiday, "By gosh and begorra," as her Grandpa Dickinson used to say, "We are all gonna get a treat," she said out loud, to no one in particular.

Humming to herself, Audrey planned her holiday. Maybe down to the creek for a swim and a picnic. No, the last time they did that, Reba caught a cold. Well, the sun was shining, and it was warming up daily, but that could be another treat on another day.

Suz Hunter had been wanting some help on a quilt. That was it! She would send Dempsey over there this very afternoon and see if tomorrow would be a good day. The children could play; Christine had been moody lately. Maybe she would cheer up. Christine loved to go to Suz's house. Her daughters, Opal and Mildred, went to school with Chris. "Yes, that is what we will do. I'll have the boys hitch up the wagon right after breakfast in the morning, and we will go visit Suz."

Henry was riding to work with John Taylor, so he wouldn't need the mule. John Taylor had a Model T Ford that he was most proud of; and he didn't seem to mind stopping by for Henry. They hoped next year to have a car. Henry's old truck had finally died, and it was too expensive to fix. Wouldn't that be something? The White family with a car—that thought lingered way too long. *I need to get started!*

"Christine, are you all through with the beds?"

"Yes, Momma."

"Good, lets get them sheets on to wash first, then we will put on a pot of soup for supper."

Christine continued changing the beds, talking to herself as she worked. "Momma washes the same every week, and every week she explains why." Just changing the beds Momma's way made sense on wash day, because then they only had five sheets to wash instead of ten.

First, the sheets went into the pot, while one of the girls stirred them around. Then it was up and down on the washboard a few times, and on to another tub with clean water to rinse.

They used to use only lye soap that Audrey made herself; but now with Henry working in the mines, they were able to buy detergent.

Christine's sensitive nose was certainly glad.

Their stir stick was Henry's old ax handle. There were two rinse tubs, and after the second rinse the clothes were run through a hand-turned wringer. That was Marie's job to turn the handle. Audrey and Chris shook out the sheets and hung them up to dry on the clothesline, and when that was full, they hung them on the bushes and on the barbed-wire fence. A family this size needed lots of places to hang clothes to dry. After the sheets, then the towels, white clothes, girl's dresses, boy's shirts. Last, the boys jeans and Henry's overalls.

Audrey's system went well, but it was still an all day job. Once the clothes were all washed, the laundry system had to be taken apart, rinsed, and put back in the wash house.

The part Chris hated the most came next, take the clothes down, fold, iron, and put away. They had three irons, which were set on the stove to get hot. As one cooled down, Chris would reach for a hot one and continue.

Chris ironed while Marie babysat the two little ones, who by this time of day were usually asleep on a quilt, either spread out on the floor close to Audrey or outside under a shade tree.

Today as they ironed, Audrey told Christine about her plans for tomorrow. They decided if Dempsey came back with good news, they would open up some apple preserves and peaches they had put up last year and make fried pies to take with them.

Suz was delighted, and she sent Dempsey home with a jar of fresh preserves she and Granny Hunter had just finished putting up that morning. "Tell your Momma to just get herself and them babies on over here. Granny and I need some company."

* * * * *

Suz only lived about three miles away, but Audrey tried to make it into a real adventure for the little ones. She would think up games for the children to play as they bounced along in the wagon.

She would have one of the boys jump down off the wagon and run ahead, hiding in the bushes. Then the little ones would try to spot them as they drove by. This game usually managed to leave them all in laughter, since cows, pigs, dogs, and even tree stumps were mistaken for Dempsey and Harvey.

The boys really didn't want to go to Suz's, so Audrey dropped them off at their Uncle Bart's with a promise to pick them up about four. Charles wanted to stay and kept giving Audrey pleading looks, but Audrey said no.

"No, the last time I left you, you and Marshall killed Uncle Bart's favorite rooster! This time you can go with the girls and me. You can play with your sisters!"

"Oh, Momma, they are just babies!" Charles whined.

"Charles, that is enough. Now sit down and sing with us."

"It's your turn Reba. Pick us out a new song to sing. If this mule doesn't get a move on, we're never gonna' get there anyway."

Reba picked "She'll Be Comin' Round the Mountains." After several choruses they finally topped the last little rise; and there was Suz waiting on them.

"Audrey, honey, do you feel okay? You look a little pale to me." Suz was looking at her with her doctor's concern look.

"I'm fine, Suz; it's the new baby. This one just seems to zap my strength."

"New baby? Audrey, you didn't tell me you and Henry were expecting again."

"Well, I haven't told Christine and the other children yet. Chris really gets upset every time I have a new little one. You know, Suz, it's her age. She's fifteen now and almost grown. It won't be long till she starts a family of her own. But for now she resents all these extra bodies. They get in the way of her privacy, of which she has none. But then who does?"

"I know, Audrey, my girls are growing up on me, too. Every baby is a gift from God, and I hope you are as excited about this one as you were the others."

"I am, Suz, and so is Henry. You know how he loves babies; it's just that I really don't seem like myself this time. Loving Henry and having his children was the best decision I ever made. Just as I was. That was the way Henry took me, and I don't think he has ever been sorry. I know I haven't"

* * * * *

Audrey was just a little over four months pregnant with her ninth child; and, secretly, she hoped her last. She was thirty-four now, and she felt that was old enough to be through with having babies.

The day of her holiday, she and Suz put their heads together and figured this latest baby would be born sometime in early September—maybe on Charles's birthday. God, she hoped not; one Charles was enough.

Suz said it was too early to predict the sex just yet, but in her heart she felt like it was another little girl.

Faye was going to be two soon, and she was her little Indian maiden. She looked so much like Henry and his mother; pure black hair and dark eyes, a real little beauty. It was hard to tell that Faye and Reba were sisters, but they were and the best of playmates. Reba, who was two years older, favored her mother more with her platinum colored hair and her green eyes.

Then there was Charles, a daddy's boy through and through and so full of it. Audrey remembered that was what her grandmother Dickinson used to say about Wesley. "That boy is just full of it." Marie was almost ten and already cooking and baby-sitting. She was a big help when you could keep her nose out of a book or from lining up her little sisters to play school. The boys seemed like men to her more and more. She rarely saw them. They hired themselves out to the farmers surrounding them.

"Thank you, God, things aren't so bad when you have family and friends." She was thankful for her family, each and every one.

I feel like an old woman.
I don't want to wipe noses,
change diapers, and wash clothes
for a bunch of kids.

—Christine White

CHAPTER TWENTY-SIX

Christine gritted her teeth, trying hard to keep the tears from flowing down her cheeks. She was shaking not from being cold, but from anger and shock. She had just walked in on her mother bathing, which in itself was not a big deal; in such a small house with so many children, somebody was always walking in on someone.

Audrey looked up to see Christine's shocked face full of tears, and instinctually she covered herself. Not her full breasts but the rounded mound of her stomach. Yes, she was pregnant again. Not that she had tried to hide the fact, but her clothing was loose, and it wasn't a topic you discussed. With eight living children and two miscarriages, Audrey didn't often get excited, especially over something as common place as another pregnancy.

"Christine, I'm sorry you found out this way, but it is certainly nothing to cry about." Audrey continued to dress, taking time to comb her long, strawberry blonde hair, shaping it into a bun on the nape of her neck.

"But, why, Momma, I don't understand why? Isn't eight children enough? Another mouth to feed, another baby to worry over." The tears really flowing now, she turned her back from the sight she did not want to see.

From outside, Chris could hear Marie's singsong voice as she sang to Faye and Reba. They were in the new swing Daddy had hung up at the end of the porch. It was the new attraction for all the children.

Charles was playing Indians by himself, every now and then trying to scare the girls with a war whoop.

Harvey was weeding the garden, and Dempsey was gathering eggs. Billy had gone off with Ezra Picket to work at his place.

Eight, she mentally counted eight heads. What would happen when, or if, Daddy got laid off and had to draw his pennies. What then? Money never lasted now.

Pennies, a name associated with unemployment checks. When there was a lay off in the mines, the general complaint was the lack of money. Pennies seemed to be the correct name for the money they received, for it certainly didn't seem like dollars.

Audrey watched Christine closely, guessing her thoughts. "Chris, I didn't ask God for another mouth to feed. He chose to give each of you to your father and me. We will manage. This baby will somehow find his or her place in this family. Are you honestly not going to welcome this baby?"

Chris heard her but was so wrapped up in her own pitiful feelings she didn't respond. The tears came again, this time Audrey lost her patience.

"Chris, if you're going to stand here and squall, go to the garden and cut okra, I saw some new pods this morning! Put your bonnet on. You know how you sunburn." Audrey turned away from Christine and began picking up Henry's discarded socks from the night before. Her barefoot boy had to wear shoes and socks in the mines. That brought a smile to Audrey's face, once again remembering their first meeting.

Ignoring Christine, Audrey went out on the porch, picked up Faye, and placed her in her lap as she joined Reba and Marie in the swing. This was better. These three had little to upset their world. She even sang along with Marie, which made the little ones laugh.

Christine hated working in the garden. She hated cutting okra most of all, and her Mother knew that. She usually was allowed to work in the house, while her mother and the boys tended the garden.

But today she decided the further away from the house she was the better she would like it. "I hope they all disappear while I'm gone!"

This had to be the blackest day of her life. How could it get any worse? She felt cheated. It wasn't the days of school she had to miss helping her Mother with sick babies. She was no student, so she didn't mind not going. It was just that life was catching up with her.

Last week she had told her best friend Opal, "I feel like an old woman with four kids. I don't want to keep babies, wipe noses, change diapers, and wash clothes!"

At fifteen Chris had a couple of suitors. Her lack of interest and deep fear of being like her mother, with too many children, kept her at arms length of anyone who might really become important to her.

* * * * *

Leaving the little ones to their swing, Audrey strolled back into the house. She would work on her sewing. She had watched Christine go to the garden and thought she might just need some time away from Christine's glaring eyes too.

She had been working for a week now on a special dress for Chris. The two of them had pored over the Sears catalog for days before deciding on the dress Chris wanted. She could make her own patterns by just looking at the pictures. Actually, she made all their clothes, even ordering denim for Henry and the boys.

She saved the material from all her flour and fertilizer sacks for clothing for the girls and herself and for shirts for the boys and Henry. But sometimes, as a special treat, they were able to buy material from the rolling store.

This dress was bought material, and if she cut it right, there would be enough left over for Reba to have a dress too. She had ordered four yards of material with bright red apples on it. This one would be Marie's because she loved red. And there, too, if she were frugal with the pattern she chose there might be enough left to make something for Faye. She saved all the scraps for the next quilt. Nothing went to waste.

The dress for Christine was going well, so Audrey decided to work on it some more while she thought about Chris and her tears that morning. In her heart she knew how Chris felt. There was a burden placed on Christine, as the oldest, to help with all the others. Audrey wanted her to feel special and have as much as she could give her, but with so many and the individual needs of each one, she knew Christine got lost in the shuffle.

* * * * *

All the new clothes were for the third Sunday in May, which was Decoration Day at Rock Creek Church, the church she and Henry were married at. Every church in the area had their special Decoration Day. It usually started in May and went through June. Labeled as the first Sunday in June, or at Rock Creek Church the third Sunday in May, it was a reunion time with relatives.

It was Decoration Day, and to the country people it was more important than Easter. The church members and previous church members
from miles around all came together to decorate the graves of their
families. They placed white sand on the grave mounds and smoothed it
upward into an inverted <u>V</u>. In the bright sun the sand just shimmered.
Audrey loved watching the sand glitter in the bright sunlight.

Lunch on the grounds, with everyone visiting and socializing with
old friends and family. Even if you went to another church, you
showed up on decoration Sunday, if not for church service than right
afterwards, since nothing got started until about one o'clock. You
usually had time to have the morning services at your own church then
go to the Decoration Day at the church your family and friends were
buried at.

The women brought flowers and food. The makeshift tables were
loaded down with all kinds of food, canned pickles, fried pies, lots of
fried chicken, cakes—anything to tempt the appetite.

Flowers were made from everything from tissue paper to pages of
the latest catalog. Fresh flowers were everywhere too. Each grave
sported one or several arrangements. Families spent weeks making
their bouquets and getting ready for the big day.

Audrey and Christine had done the same. They had gathered fruit
jars and made arrangements to go in them. Audrey had taken scraps of
material, tying them together in the center, pulling the pieces forward
until they resembled a flower. Using this same method she fashioned
other flowers with tissue paper and with paper from the catalogs.

* * * * *

Now she was trying to finish all the new dresses she had started for
the girls. With such a big family, every day could be a sewing day. Aunt
Viola had given her the Singer treadle machine she used. Uncle
Abraham had bought Viola a new one, for, like Audrey, she had to sew
a lot for her large family.

Christine wandered back into the house, stopping in the kitchen to
put the okra down. Feeling bad now that she had upset her mother, but
not yet ready to make amends, she started fussing around the kitchen.

"Momma, is it okay if I make some soup for lunch? There's some
left over stew meat, and I can use some of the canned vegetables from

last year?" There were always vegetables, fresh and canned. She could even make some cornbread and fry up those awful pods of okra.

Audrey heard her banging around in the kitchen, but decided to let her work it out in her own way.

"Fine, Chris, that sounds good. Fry up some okra too." That would probably keep those pans banging a little longer.

She wouldn't need her for another hour or so to try on the dress. Once it was fitted and pinned up, then Chris could hem the dress, and she would start on the next one.

I hope she likes this dress as much as she did the picture in the catalog.

Humming to herself, thinking it would be nice to do something special for Christine, Audrey remembered the piece of material Viola had given her on their last visit. It wasn't large enough for a dress, but maybe a skirt. Chris would like that. She would see what she could do with that, just as soon as she finished all these Decoration Day clothes. Some days there was just too much to do.

***** *****

Finally all the new clothes were finished, and they were all dressed for their day at Rock Creek. Henry surveyed them all and had a comment for every one.

"Marie, those are the reddest apples I have ever seen." Marie just beamed, for she thought it was certainly the prettiest dress she had ever owned. The apples made it special.

The four yards of material Audrey purchased from the traveling store were well worth the smile on Marie's face.

"Christine, you look prettier than a new born calf." Christine laughed at her Daddy's choice of words for a compliment. Only grinning at Christine's reaction Henry continued. "You and your momma did a real nice job on your dress."

Christine's dress had small blue flowers on it, and as a finishing touch Audrey had made a beautiful white collar.

Reba twirled around so Henry would notice how her pink dress spread out as she turned. She was a vision with her hair up in a pink bow. He picked her up and told her what a beauty she was.

Faye, at two, didn't know what all was happening, but it looked like fun, so she tried to imitate Reba. She spun around ending up in a heap in the floor, but her little dress, a replica of Marie's, was very pretty.

"Faye, you are a sight to behold too," Henry said, grabbing her up and starting toward the door.

Not to be outdone the boys pushed and shoved each other until Henry noticed them too. "You boys look all spit polished and ready to go somewhere. Got a date or something?"

Grinning at each other, with Billy turning a little pink the minute dating was mentioned, they trouped outside to wait on the girls.

Henry stopped in the doorway. He was not an emotional man, but the sight of his beautiful family put tears in his eyes. Turning around he placed his arm around Audrey, as he looked at each child. "Sug, you did good, and you look pretty enough to pinch yourself."

God knew he was proud of his family. The size of it was even better; he didn't care if there was always a new baby. He liked babies. To hold that thought, he gave Faye another hug and kiss.

"Okay, young'uns get yourselves out the door and in the truck."

The car Audrey had been dreaming about turned out to be a flatbed truck. With such a large family they couldn't all fit in a car, or at least that was what Henry had told her when he came home with another truck. He had built sideboards and benches in the back of the truck, so all but Faye were allowed to sit in the back.

Christine hated riding in the back. She spent hours on her hair and did not want the wind messing up her best efforts. Knowing how she felt, Audrey said, "Chris you can set up front with your Daddy and me. You can hold Faye."

The boys jousted with each other trying to get in but were still careful not to mess up their new shirts. Audrey had let them wear their jeans, but each had a new shirt.

Actually Audrey agreed with Henry. They had a very attractive family. And like the children, she was anxious to get to the church and visit with all her friends and family. She knew Uncle Abraham and Aunt Viola would be there. Maybe they had some news about Olivet.

"Let's go, Henry, I can't wait any longer." Audrey thought Henry was certainly slow on this special day.

"Okay, Sug. Is everybody ready?" With the chorus of young voices urging him on, Henry hit the gas, and they were on their way.

Aunt Audrey, I done got my
tater baked with those
Army folks. I ain't got
no Uncle Sam in my family.

—Marshall White

CHAPTER TWENTY-SEVEN

Marshall was A.W.O.L. Bud and Vertie were beside themselves in frustration with the boy. He was just plain uncontrollable! He simply, "Didn't wanta' go." Uncle Sam wanted Marshall, but Marshall didn't want no part of Uncle Sam's Army.

Audrey always said Charles was just another Marshall, headstrong and wild. Thank goodness he was still too young to have to go. She had enough troubles just keeping that boy in school. She tried; they all tried. With a push and a shove, you could get him on the school bus, but at the next stop he would get off. Harvey and Dempsey would try to keep him on the bus, but more times than not he escaped them and came back home.

The first time Marshall separated himself from the Army, he showed up at Audrey's front door. Billy and Harvey saw him first and stashed him out in the barn. Audrey wondered why they all of a sudden seemed so industrious, working in the barn, cleaning and stacking hay. Everyday it was something new. Some new reason they needed to go to the barn and have an extra biscuit or piece of cornbread to take along on this short trip to the barn.

"Henry, those boys are up to something. I feel it."

"Now, Sug, let those boys alone; they work hard, and they need to have some fun." Henry was always in favor of a little fun.

"That's just it, Henry, they do work hard, so why are they wanting to work some more? Just don't seem natural—not for those two boys. I tell you, they are up to something!"

Audrey was right. The M.P.s finally showed up. First they went to Vertie and Bud's house, finally finding their way to Henry and Audrey's. Not taking anyone's word, especially a couple of guilty looking boys, they searched for him, and with Charles two steps behind them. Billy and Harvey walked circles in the front yard as the M.P.s started toward the barn.

Audrey would have bet money that they would find him in the barn, but if he was there they didn't turn him up.

Charles was skipping around the M.P.s as they came out of the barn, never saying a word, which in itself was unusual; for Charles was never at a loss for words.

He was looking like the cat who swallowed the canary, bright eyed and grinning from ear to ear.

Audrey held her breath when they point blank asked Billy Hugh if he knew where Marshall was.

"Marshall, oh, yes, Marshall. Harvey," he continued, "Harvey, didn't Marshall go hunting with us just last month?" Billy turned and looked at Harvey, as if he really needed an answer to his question.

"Sure did, Billy Hugh," Harvey spoke up very quickly, too quickly for Audrey.

"Yep, that's right, we went up on the ridge. Them dogs like to run our legs off. Thought sure they was running a deer. That Marshall like to have croaked when they treed that ol' possum. Yep, ol' Marshall was a sight for sore eyes."

"Son," the M.P. said patiently, "I asked you if Marshall White was here, now?"

"As I was a-sayin' officer, Marshall and me and some of the boys, we all went a-huntin' last month. We also took ourselves a little fishin' trip..." Billy talked non-stop for five minutes; all about his and Marshall's last hunting trip and he had just started on their fishing trip when the officer said, "Never mind!"

"Ma'am, I know that boy is here somewhere, but I believe you when you tell me you haven't seen him. I'm gonna' have my boys search for him in the house next. I don't figure we are going to find him, but, ma'am, when he shows himself, please send him on back. Okay? Uncle Sam don't take kindly to deserters, ma'am."

After that long speech, Audrey just nodded her head. She planned on turning a few stones herself as soon as these fellows left, starting with Billy Hugh and Harvey.

True to his word, the M.P. did, indeed, search the house. Finding no sign of Marshall, he started to leave, but in military fashion spoke one more word of caution, "Send him on back, ma'am, when he turns up. Uncle Sam wants that boy! Thank you for all your cooperation, Miz White."

The M.P. had no more than got out of the lane until Audrey started. "Billy Hugh, Harvey, get over here, now." That was Audrey's you-don't-dare-not-do-what-I-say voice. "Where are you hiding Marshall?"

"Now, Momma, don't go and get all upset," Billy Hugh said. "They don't know for sure he is here."

"But I know for sure he is here somewhere. Billy Hugh, I did not ask you if he was here. I asked you where you were hiding him?"

"Aw, Momma."

"Billy Hugh White!"

"Momma, I swear he was in the barn. Momma, you know Marshall ain't ready for the Army!" Billy was talking fast trying to appease her. He was tall for his age, a good head taller than his momma was, but when she spoke he still listened, just as he did as a small boy. He knew his momma didn't take to lying, and she certainly didn't take no sassing. Billy figured he would have to find Marshall himself in order to satisfy her.

"Billy, if he was in the barn, they would have found him. There aren't that many places to hide out there." Audrey told him as calmly as she could.

"Momma, I tell you that's where we left him," Billy said a little puzzled by the situation himself.

"Harvey, do you know anything about this?"

"No, ma'am!" Harvey spoke up real fast.

Harvey could lie better than anyone, but Audrey didn't feel like that was the case this time.

"Where could he be?" she asked no one in particular. About that time she caught sight of Charles out of the corner of her eye. He was still skipping around. "Okay, young man, what do you know about all this?"

"Who me?"

"Yes, you! Talk!"

"I saw him go in the house, Momma, a-fore them fellows got here," Charles spoke up really fast.

With that statement still ringing in the air, Billy and Harvey made a dash for the house, landing on the front porch steps at the same time, almost knocking each other down.

By the time Audrey and the rest of the family got in the house, they could hear Marshall yelling, but they couldn't see him. Evidently Billy and Harvey were having the same problem.

"Marshall, where are you?" Billy yelled.

"Yeah," chimed in Harvey, "Momma's mad as an old wet hen!"

"Billy Hugh, get me out of here. I'm stuck in this damned ol' chimney'." Marshall was yelling at the same time Billy and Harvey were shoving each other aside, both trying to get to him first.

Sure enough, he was stuck in the fireplace. When he had spotted the M.P.s, he went into the house and climbed up in the chimney. The only problem was he got his pants stuck on a nail or something and couldn't get back down. Before Billy and Harvey managed to get him out of there, Audrey was laughing so hard she was crying.

Standing in front of Audrey were, in truth, three young men, all looking a little sheepish; but she was only talking to one of them. "Marshall White, what is your problem? Don't you know you can't just leave the Army whenever you up and feel like it?"

Grinning like a possum, Marshall said, "Aunt Audrey, I just got my tater baked on that Army stuff. I'd rather be here with the boys."

With that Audrey turned around and marched into the kitchen, where she collapsed into laughter again.

The boys stood where they were, looking at each other, not really knowing what they should do next. Marshall couldn't decide if Audrey was really mad or just temporarily not mad. He could still hear her laughter long after she left the room. Maybe they should just all go outside and not bother her anymore. About the time he was going to make that suggestion, Henry walked in the door, filling the doorway with his size. There was no leaving the room at that point for anyone.

"What's going on here? Howdy, Marshall, heard you decided to quit the Army. Where's your momma, Charles?" Henry's questions came out one on top of the other.

Getting only a nod toward the kitchen from Charles and at a loss for what to do, he left the room in search of Audrey.

In short order, she had him set straight about the goings-on. As she finished her speech, the three young men in question appeared in the kitchen. Audrey, taking charge as usual, with Christine's help, served them all supper; then she politely showed Marshall the door.

"Marshall you and the Army have got to make peace sooner or later, but for right now go see your momma and daddy."

"Yes, Aunt Audrey. Thanks for supper. I always say you are the best cook in the whole world."

Audrey just shook her head as she watched Marshall walking down the road, whistling as he went, taking time to pick up a stick to throw for old Shep to fetch. "That boy ain't got a care in the world. He ain't never going to grow up. Even Uncle Sam can't help him," Audrey said, laughing to herself as she turned and went back in the house to straighten out a couple of her own "not a care in the world" young men.

* * * * *

Audrey was right about Marshall and Uncle Sam. Marshall went back and left again, almost as soon as he got there. This time they almost caught him at a church party. He told them later how an M.P. was within touching distance of him, as he was hiding in a bush.

Marshall stayed home a month that time before they came to get him. This time Uncle Sam had finally had enough of Marshall too! Uncle Sam called it quits! They threw him in the brig for six weeks then sent him home with a dishonorable discharge.

Marshall had his tater baked, but then so did Uncle Sam. With his usual grin, Marshall took it all in stride, coming over to Audrey and Henry's house, hunting and fishing with the boys, always staying long enough to eat Audrey's good cooking. It was almost as if he had never been gone.

You have to face
life and death head on.
God didn't provide us a place
to hide. He gave us a place to live.

—Abraham Dickinson

CHAPTER TWENTY-EIGHT

It was a cold, damp, almost totally engulfing cold coming from within. As Audrey lay there in bed in a tight knot, her arms crossed protectively in front of her, the covers pulled up well over her head; she tried to reconstruct the past week and tried to understand within herself how this could be. Where was this coming from. Why? How? How could she feel so empty and cold inside, a truly physical cold? Her brain wouldn't work, even simple ideas that formed couldn't be answered. What had she done today? Who had she seen? What had she eaten for supper? Nothing, she felt nothing!

Audrey often wondered if there were others like her. People who went within, heard voices, and had dreams. Dreams and voices that seemed to speak the truth, then things she thought of or imagined that would happen, just like she had imagined they would.

Maybe she had an overactive imagination. Was that what it was? She had heard that spoken about, but was that her? She didn't know. She only knew she was seldom lonely or scared. Her voices were always there. They consoled her. They told her not to be frightened and that it would be okay as it always was.

Audrey always got answers, for better or worse. Listen—just listen—she would think; be very still, and you'll know what to do. Things change, you can't go back. The future is there, and you must go forward.

Only this time she did remember, and she did want to go back. Yes, it probably was a week ago or maybe more. She remembered it all now—every horrible moment.

Audrey had gotten up long before dawn. She was restless, trying to be quiet so as not to wake Henry and the children. She slipped out on the front porch, quietly sliding into her rocking chair. She wouldn't rock; she would just sit there until the dream went away. The dreams were back, coming more often. Uncle Abraham had told her to try sleeping with the Bible under her head. She had tried that, but it didn't help; nor did the water bowl that someone else had thought was a cure for dreams. Nothing helped, she knew things she didn't want to know. There was something wrong with Billy Hugh, she just knew it, but couldn't tell you how or why.

He had been down in Walker County for several weeks now, working for this one and that one, trying not to be a burden to her and Henry.

After all, he was a grown man now; and he and Henry had words the last time he was home. Something Billy said had gotten Henry stirred up, and before she knew it, she was between the two of them begging them both to stop. Billy left after that, and she wasn't able to talk to him, to tell him how very much she loved him.

She just knew there was something wrong with him. Hadn't she dreamed it three nights in a row. She had seen it clear as day, Billy lying on the ground hurt.

Should she wake Henry? "No!" He hated her dreams almost as much as she did. They never seemed to be happy dreams, always deaths anymore. She shuddered, just mentioning death made her do that.

Billy was in trouble, and as far as she knew, he hadn't even been sick. Henry would think she was crazy, but they needed to go to him. Walker County was a good hour away. What if they were too late?

Her mind started to wander. *Did all the children have clean clothes? What could she fix to take with them?*

"Audrey, stop this!" she said to herself. "It was only a dream, for heaven's sakes." She halfway convinced herself, at least for the moment. It was then that she saw the headlights coming over the ridge. Most people weren't up and stirring about this early. *Bad news, I suppose,* she thought to herself. Well they were still a-ways off. They still had to go down a holler and up another hill before getting to them.

She watched a few minutes longer but couldn't seem to sit still. She walked to the edge of the porch, sitting down on the top step. She wished she had a cigarette. The country gentlemen sack was on the mantle. She only allowed herself three cigarettes a day. Besides she would have to go back in the house and risk waking Henry and the children. She guessed the cigarette would wait.

The smell of the lilac bush was really strong, it seemed to lay very heavy in the cool morning air. Most days she welcomed the smell, but today it reminded her of the day Renee had died. The mums were still in bloom that year. They had smelled so good, and then in moments Renee had been gone. She had picked flowers that day for the table. For as long as she lived, she would think of Renee and death when she smelled the sweet odor of flowers, especially when it was such a strong, lingering odor. She had to stop this. Her thoughts were running away with her.

The car continued. Now she could hear the sound of the engine. Before she could turn around to go back inside, Henry was standing beside her.

"Sug, what is it? Another bad dream?" Henry who was slipping his arms into his shirt was looking at Audrey questioningly, waiting for an answer.

"Yes, the same one."

Audrey turned back toward the front yard just as the car pulled in. "Bad news?" Henry questioned as he looked into her eyes. Audrey started to cry before John William and Haskel White had turned the motor off. Henry looked at her and then walked out to the car.

"Mornin', boys. Up and about a little early, ain't you?" Henry asked as he nodded toward Haskel and shook John's hand.

"Yes sir, we just rode in from Walker County. It's your boy, Billy Hugh. He's in bad shape. There was a logging accident, and Bill was in the middle of it. Seems he was riding in a logging truck when the load shifted. Bill landed on the bottom. He's alive Henry, but we don't know for how long."

Henry turned to look at Audrey, wondering how much of that conversation she had heard. Then seeing her crumbled up on the floor, he knew she either heard it all or had known all along.

"You boys come on in." Henry said as he ran on up to the porch, sitting down beside Audrey, pulling her into his arms. She was very pregnant. It was almost time, and he worried how this news would affect her and the baby.

"Audrey, honey, I'll go get him and bring him home. He has to be okay. Maybe it's not as bad as the boys think." Audrey just nodded. She couldn't say anything; she was remembering so much, like the day he was born, his learning to walk, talk, so much to remember.

As Henry got ready, Audrey pulled herself together and put the coffee on.

167

John looked at her closely, "Aunt Audrey, did you know? It looked like you were waiting on us."

"Yes, I knew, I was about to wake Henry when I saw your car lights."

"I'm sorry, Aunt Audrey. I sure hope he is okay."

"I know, John, I know."

Haskel just looked at them and shook his head. The family all knew about Audrey and her dreams and signs, but it distressed her so much, they didn't ask or push her on the subject.

"Ready, boys?" Henry asked. "Sug, you gonna be all right?" She nodded. "The baby?" He questioned. It seemed like there was always another baby.

"It's okay Henry. He or she seems to be sleeping or is just being still out of respect."

"Okay, Sug, it's going to be okay. I woke Harvey and Charles up. I'm taking Charles with me. That should make things a little easier here." Henry spoke as he continued buttoning his shirt.

He gave her a hug and turned to go. "Henry, tell Billy Hugh I love him." Audrey spoke, almost in a whisper. Billy had to know she loved him no matter what happened.

Charles, bright eyed and full of energy, was hopping around on one foot, trying to get his other shoe on as he moved to the door.

Christine came from the girls' room with a bewildered look on her face, but automatically helped Charles get his shoe on. Thinking to herself, *more bad news.* Seemed like it was always something.

Audrey handed Henry a cup of coffee and Charles a cold biscuit almost in the same motion. In a flurry they were gone with Charles hanging out the window yelling. "Bye, Momma; bye, Chris; Momma, I lost my knife; Momma, find my knife."

His Uncle Bart had given him a knife the day they went to Suz Hunter's on their outing. Bart had thought it would keep him from feeling so bad since Audrey wouldn't let him stay at Bart's house with the older boys. She turned and walked back in the house, picking up Charles's knife off the porch rail as she went in to face four sleepy children.

"What is it, Momma?" Marie asked, "what's wrong?"

Marie, her most curious child, always wanted an answer for everything. "Billy is sick, Daddy has gone to check on him." Audrey spoke as if in a dream, she did not want to express all her thoughts concerning Billy.

Marie, satisfied with that answer, walked over to the chair where she had left her dolls the night before. Picking her favorite one up, she crawled up on the couch and went back to sleep.

There would be no sleep for Audrey or Chris, they knew that something was really wrong.

Henry was gone all day and well into the night, but finally John brought him and Charles home, and behind them in a truck was Billy Hugh, who was known by one and all as Bill White, just like his Grandpa, Will, had called him so many years ago.

Billy was dead. Billy, just coming into the prime of his life, gone. Billy Hugh White left this world as quietly as he entered. Henry, his earthly father by a strange twist of fate, brought him home, just as he promised Audrey he would.

Audrey knew the morning Henry and Charles had left to go see about Billy that she would not see her son alive again, but there is always a slim thread of hope as long as one does not see the end results.

Billy was dead. She must accept that, and with the body there in her home she would.

Henry brought him home in a simple, wooden casket which rested on the back of a logging truck. Not procedural, but perhaps prophetic of the way Billy lived and died.

Billy loved the woods, any portion of the woods; hunting, fishing, trapping, or logging. It thrilled him to work in the woods.

The accident was just that, a horrible accident, but to Audrey a devastation that she could not readily get over.

The casket was placed on two sawhorses in the living room, draped in black. Candles and oil lamps were lit around the room. The casket would remain for two days while the White family paid their respects to a much beloved son.

During the first night of Billy's return, well past the time for a neighbor to stop by to pay respects, there was a quiet knock at the door. Henry, who was sitting up with his brother Bart, had been softly talking to Bart about Billy and the things they had done. Audrey was in an adjoining room, finally asleep after Dr. Stanley had been summoned to give her a sedative to help her.

Bart stood up and opened the door. Standing on the other side was Eugene Godwin. Bart turned around to see Henry's reaction. It was Henry's home—would he want this particular intrusion? Henry stood up and simply motioned for Eugene to come in.

"Hello, Gene. Come in. I think it would please Billy Hugh to know that you came."

"Henry, I did not know if I would be welcome or not, but I wanted to say, I'm sorry."

"Thank you, Gene, it is a difficult time for all of us. Please come on in."

Eugene and Henry shook hands and stood side-by-side looking down at Billy. Bart, considered a very strong man by most people, turned away from the sight in tears.

Two fathers. Two very real fathers, one in name only and the other a true father in every sense of the word, standing side-by-side paying respects to their son.

"Gene, would you like to sit awhile with me and Bart?"

"Henry, I thank you for asking me, but Gladys June does not know that I came. I only told her I had to run over to a neighbor's house to return something. I'm sure my vague reason for leaving has unnerved her, but I had to come."

"I understand, I will tell Audrey tomorrow that you came."

"Henry, perhaps, you shouldn't tell her, I don't want to add anything to the grief she is already experiencing." With that Thaddeus Eugene Godwin walked out of Billy's life for the second time.

Bart and Henry discussed the new turn of events and decided Gene was correct in his thinking; they would not tell Audrey he came.

Billy was buried in a very simple ceremony at Rock Creek Cemetery. The funeral was nothing even close to the one Purvey had. Audrey, not able to make any decisions had left everything up to Henry and their family and friends, who decided the best thing for Audrey would be simplicity and to place Billy in his final resting place as quickly as possible.

As word spread, the Dickinson and White families began to gather. Abraham was summoned; he took charge, conducting a very simple graveside service. With love and grace he praised God for this young man who had brought joy to so many.

Henry, Audrey, and all their children were there along with the very immediate families. Very few neighbors came to the service, but as was tradition, several families baked and cooked, bringing food to the home for the family. After the service everyone went home with

Henry and Audrey, trying in their own way to comfort the family. A tragedy such as this one brought families together, and Billy's life was spoken about over and over again.

It was later that day when Audrey could no longer deal with what life had brought her. It was easier to withdraw and not face any of the harsh facts that were going on around her.

Speaking only to herself and only in her heart, Audrey said, "Okay, that's enough. You will get up from here and go on. There's been far too many days in this oblivion."

She knew the words she spoke to herself were wise and true, yet the actions she needed her body to do would not come. She was determined to climb out of this bed—pick up the pieces of her life and go on. The other children needed her. The others, yes the others needed her, Henry and the children. Where was Henry? Now that she had decided she would get up, where was everyone?

Oh, but it was hard to let go of Billy. She couldn't speak the words out loud. They hurt too much. Billy was gone, dead. She remembered, or thought she did, a house full of people around her. Suz was there, maybe Vertie and Jean. Paralee? Yes, now she remembered Paralee was there. She had wanted to take Faye and Reba with her, but Henry. No Henry would never stand up to his momma. It had to be Suz or Vertie, they told her no!

Now Audrey was laughing. Just the very thought of someone telling Paralee no! The laughter bubbled out of her, uncontrollably. She laughed and laughed. Laughter and tears. Her whole life had been a lot of both.

Billy, born out of a tragic happening in her life, who had brought such joy to her was gone. Now she had to get up and go on. It was the laughter that brought the family she had been wondering about to the door of her room. For days they had listened to her cry. She had sobbed Billy's name; and though they had all tried to console her, Audrey had drifted off into her own thoughts in her own world. This was the first sign of life coming from that room.

"Oh, Vertie, did someone really tell Paralee no?" Audrey's laughter was contagious.

Now, Vertie laughing with tears running down her face, was nodding yes and pointing to Suz. "It was Suz. She said no. Oh Audrey it was so good to hear. I tried not to laugh then. Henry and Bud ran out the door on some errand the minute Suz said no, so Paralee couldn't get them to help."

"Audrey, Suz had her hands on her hips and she wasn't budging." Jean was looking at Suz, describing with her own hands resting on her hips the way Suz looked. Now that Audrey was back with them, everyone was talking at once.

Maybe Momma's having another baby.
You know she was awful
sick with Barbara Jean.

—Marie White

CHAPTER TWENTY-NINE

Henry was in the field plowing the new garden when the first dizzy spell and sudden cramps hit Audrey.

Where were those young'uns' when you needed one? Audrey wondered, If she didn't need them they would be right under foot.

It had been a stormy couple of days, and after being cooped up in the house, they were all ready to run and play, whoop and holler. Actually it was Charles' hollering at Reba that finally caught Audrey's attention.

The pain was intense, but after a few moments she had her bearings and moved toward the sounds, stopping only minutes at a time as wave after wave of pain hit her. This was something new. The dull cramps of childbirth she knew, but this was different.

Just as she had given up hope of attracting Charles or Reba's attention, Marie ran through the front door. She was in search of an old doll for some game she was playing, most likely school. That child loved to boss and teach her dolls, or her sisters when they would sit still for it.

"Momma, what's wrong?" Marie screamed as Audrey slumped to the floor.

Barely able to speak, she reached for Marie's hand and whispered, "Get your daddy."

"Oh, Momma, I don't want to leave you. You look awful."

"Just get your daddy, Marie. I'll be fine."

Marie ran out the back door yelling for Christine, who was in the wash house.

From the screeching she was doing, Chris figured Marie had been stung by a bee or Charles had clobbered her with a stick. The usual little upsets for a Saturday morning.

Gasping for breath, Marie kept saying, "Get Daddy! Get Daddy—Mama's real sick! Real sick!"

* * * * *

Henry was plowing the damp earth and very thankful for the dampness. It not only felt good to his bare feet, but it sure did make plowing a lot easier. Sometimes the Alabama clay was so dry nothing would grow anyway. The plow fought with the hard earth, often losing the fight.

Henry couldn't hear what was going on at the house, but the flurry of activity caught his eye. Christine was waving her apron, and Charles was running towards him. Henry dropped the reins and started toward the house, only to stop in mid-flight, to turn around, and lay the plow on its side, wrapping the reins around the handle. The boys could rescue ol' Mac later.

As soon as she was satisfied that Henry was headed towards her, Christine turned and ran back to the house.

Henry grabbed Audrey up that day and put her in the truck. Leaving Chris in charge of the children, he took her to Doctor Stanley's office. Doctor C.P. Stanley had been their doctor for too many years to count. Audrey had even named Charles after him; Charles Peyton. Doctor Stanley would know what to do. Henry and Audrey both set great store by Doctor Stanley's knowledge. *Yes*, Henry thought, *Doctor Stanley will make Audrey better.*

That was the beginning. She spent three days in the hospital that time, mostly under observation. She slept the days away, out of pain, due to the medication; but Doctor Stanley did not know what was causing her distress. Nothing seemed to stack up for a true diagnosis. So finally they let her go home with instructions to Henry, "Bring her back at the first sign of anything."

Barbara Jean was their big problem for now. Audrey had been nursing her, and now with all the medication, Barbara wouldn't nurse. She wouldn't drink anything they mixed up for her. She spit up the Carnation milk with syrup. About all she was taking at the moment was sugar water. Finally, Suz suggested goat's milk. Henry drove about ten miles to even find one. First it was for a sample and then, when it worked, he went back for the goat.

Audrey was depressed; she just didn't seem to be getting better. Henry wasn't in much better shape. Audrey was their whole life. She told them all what to do, and when—including him. What on earth would they do if she had to go back to the hospital, even for a short stay?

"Henry, next week you need to get the ground ready to plant the garden."

"Christine, be sure and wash on Monday; the boys are about out of shirts. "

"Marie, go ahead and start some beans for supper."

As sick as she was, Audrey knew everything that had to be done.

In late January, Dr. Stanley suggested Henry take her to a specialist in Birmingham, the closest big city. Their old truck was okay for around town, but that long of a drive was pretty much out of the question. Audrey made the decision to go on the Greyhound Bus, and Henry had no choice but to agree.

"Audrey, I have you set up with an appointment with Doctor Wilson in Birmingham. He will see you at the hospital and run a few tests, so plan on spending the day, for I'm sure it will take several hours." Doctor Stanley made all the arrangements. He requested that Doctor Wilson bill his office, he had been Audrey's doctor through too many hardships. He felt like he should know what was wrong, but he didn't.

Early Wednesday morning, Henry took Audrey and Christine to the bus station. He promised to take care of Barbara Jean and the other children. In his heart he thought he should go with her, but he would stand by her judgement that Christine could take care of her.

The tests were long, and she was worn out by the time Dr. Wilson called them into his office to talk.

"Mrs. White, I've examined you, and I know you are in pain. There is swelling in your abdomen, and that could be from the last baby. Nine babies in nineteen years and two miscarriages have been hard on your body. You are basically healthy, and I've noted that all the births were normal. Frankly I'm stumped." Dr. Wilson shook his head, resting his hand on his chin as he continued. "I'll contact Doctor Stanley and suggest that he do exploratory surgery. Hopefully that will tell us what's wrong."

Audrey felt like the entire trip was a waste of time. Doctor Stanley had never failed her, so she would go back home and get better.

"Chris, please hand me my jacket, we need to catch that bus, your daddy will be worried, if we aren't on it.

Chris, trying to hide her tears, helped her mother into her coat, putting her arm around her to support her as they walked out of the hospital to the bus stop.

What would they do if anything happened to her mother? Chris didn't even want to think about it, but with her mother sound asleep beside her on the bus, her mind wouldn't stop asking that question.

Henry met them at the bus station with the entire family. No one wanted to stay home and wait any longer, it had been a long day for all of them.

She was home two days and the pain became so intense Henry insisted she go to the hospital. As he took her out the door, back to the hospital again, she was still giving instructions.

She had Christine take Barbara Jean to Belzie and Olivet. They had gotten married last February and didn't have any children yet. They were frequent visitors, always playing with Faye and holding Barbara Jean. They had offered to help while she was in the hospital. They were willing to take care of one or all of the children. They were staying with Evie, and she too insisted the children were welcome.

It seemed best to Audrey for the other children to stay with Christine and go on as usual. Barbara was a different story. She was little and fussy about her milk. She needed special attention—the kind Audrey was sure she would get in Olivet's household.

So with Barbara settled with Belzie and Olivet, Audrey was ready for the trip to the hospital. She was in and out of the hospital four times from January to March. She couldn't hold anything in her stomach. Already thin, she became even thinner. They gave her glucose and shots, then finally surgery, but nothing seemed to help.

On April 1st Dr. Stanley called Henry in for a little talk.

"Henry, Audrey isn't getting any better, and to be honest, we don't know any more than we did. As you know we found a small ulcer in her stomach and removed it, but that shouldn't cause all the pain she is having. To be honest, Henry I don't think she is going to pull through this unless we get a miracle."

Audrey was getting worse daily, and Dr. Stanley wanted Henry to be aware, not of just the immediate future but of the possibilities that she would not make it.

"She wants to go home." Dr. Stanley told Henry, "she can go, but," he made it clear, "she will be back."

At this point it didn't seem wise to argue with her; it was more important that she be happy. Whatever Audrey wanted was what Dr. Stanley and Henry were ready and willing to do.

So she came home; very weak, but smiling. Henry carried her into the house and placed her on their bed.

Audrey was so happy to see them all. She was smiling, laughing, and crying all at the same time.

Rowdy little Charles was being good, to everyone's surprise. The moment she was home, he brought her flower bouquets. They were very pretty, but the smell made her sick. Even so, she wouldn't allow Christine to take them out of her room. Instead she had Christine place them on the windowsill, well away from the bed.

Belzie and Olivet brought Barbara home for a visit. Audrey held her and told Faye stories. Faye lay beside her, stiller than anyone had ever seen her. You would think she was asleep, except for her little hands rubbing Audrey's arm up and down.

Marie stared at her with huge eyes and refused to leave the room. She slid down the wall ending up on the floor in a lump, never taking her eyes off her momma.

What a mess they were all in. Henry finally dragged everyone out of the room and into the kitchen. He left it up to their Aunt Stella, Bart's wife, who was a big favorite of Christine's, to tell them what he could not bring himself to do.

* * * * *

"Chris, Harvey, children, your momma is real sick," Aunt Stella began. "Real sick. Doctor Stanley let her come home so you could see her and she could see you." With the tears rolling down her work-worn face she continued. "Your mother is going to go be with Jesus. She loves you all so much, but he needs her up in heaven." Audrey, their lovely mother was dying. Audrey, who was not yet thirty-five was dying. Not Audrey, not this much loved woman. It was breaking her heart to tell them. Not knowing how to tell them, she told them in the only way she knew how. Heaven would be her resting-place. There were days that she wanted to see Heaven herself.

"Aunt Stella, maybe its another baby; you know Momma was real sick with Barbara Jean!" Marie was sure she had the answer.

"No, sweetheart, that was different. There's no baby this time. The doctors can't make her better."

Marie just looked at her as if to say "I know you are wrong, and I will prove it." Then she ran back to Audrey's room, sitting down just inside the door.

The boys never said a word. They just looked at each other and then at Henry. Dempsey was crying, and Harvey and Charles were white as sheets.

Henry, a broken man, sat slumped over the table, the very table he had made for his big and growing family. It had two long benches, one down each side with straight chairs sitting at each end.

Audrey seldom used her chair; she was always too busy serving the family, being sure they all had everything they needed.

Now that she thought about it, Chris could not remember her mother ever sitting down at the table for a complete meal.

All of a sudden, Christine started banging pots and pans, beginning supper. Thinking as she did, *How can she do this to me? I never wanted her to have all these children, and that's what is killing her. Now I will have to take care of them. No! No! No!* Out loud she didn't say anything. She continued to bang around the kitchen, preparing supper, before anyone could suggest she should do that; or God forbid someone ask her how she felt.

Aunt Stella kept talking, because she knew that in spite of the reactions she was getting, they were all listening. "Dr. Stanley is not sure what was wrong. The stomach surgery didn't work. Your mother is dehydrated and nothing they try seems to help."

She was slipping away. Audrey was in a lot of pain, although she did not and had not complained, since the first day that Henry had scooped her up and taken her through the door to the doctor.

When Chris had dinner ready, Aunt Stella was still talking. One by one she talked to each child. Every conversation was different, but they all added up to the same thing; Audrey was dying.

Reba, at five, didn't really understand what all the fuss was about.

"Honey, do you remember when your pet kitten Sammy died and went to Heaven?"

"Yes, ma'am, and he didn't come back no more."

When Aunt Stella explained to her using her kitten as an example, she began to cry, missing her mother already.

Marie was a different story. She looked straight at her Aunt Stella and told her, "You're wrong." With her ten-year-old fists clenched, she dared her Aunt Stella to continue.

It was a very long evening. Supper sat on the table untouched. Chris kept busy, and Henry kept stepping outside for a breath of fresh air, or so he said.

Wesley came over, and he and Henry had a drink. After that Henry didn't go outside anymore. He sat for hours staring at the fire, holding Faye on his lap.

About midnight Audrey called out to him. "Honey, I think I better go back to the hospital. I'm not doing so well."

"Henry, I'll stay here as long as need be, you two go on now." Stella assured them she would watch the babies.

Audrey had Henry and Christine help her out to the truck, telling Chris on the way to be strong and help Henry with the babies.

After they were gone, Christine picked up Marie from the floor. She had fallen asleep in their mother's room, never knowing she had left. Chris placed her in the bed where Audrey had spent the past several hours. Marie, restless even in her sleep, dreamed of fields full of flowers. She picked flowers for her mother in her sleep.

Chris cried herself to sleep that night, and the next three nights too.

✳ ✳ ✳ ✳ ✳

On April 6th, the day Barbara Jean was seven months old, Audrey had Doctor Stanley send word for Belzie and Olivet to come see her. Since she had been increasingly getting worse, they had continued to keep Barbara; and she wanted to talk to them about that.

Olivet leaned over the bed and kissed her on the forehead as he asked, "How are you feeling Audrey?"

"Not good, Olivet. Doctor Stanley has sorta given up on me," Audrey answered. She was very weak and spoke so softly that he continued to lean over her as she spoke. She asked him about Barbara Jean, and from the grin on his face as he told her about Barbara's trying to crawl, she knew she had made a good decision.

"Olivet, Belzie," she looked at each of them. "Henry is going to need a lot of help with the babies. Christine will have her hands full with Faye, Charles, and Reba. Barbara Jean needs lots of care. Would you, do you think you could keep her? Raise her like your own. If Henry gets married before she is two and can take her and care for her, let him. But if he can't, please take good care of her. Henry and me talked about it, and he wants to ask Christine one more time to help him with her. If she doesn't think she can, we know you will do right by her."

Belzie was crying, and so were the others in the room. It was true. They already loved the baby. They had Barbara for four of her six months, due to Audrey's illness. The whole family loved her.

They were still living with Belzie's mother, Evie, and she, like the rest of the family, already thought of Barbara Jean as a member of their family.

First Olivet, then Belzie promised her to do their very best. But they would only keep her until Audrey got on her feet and came home. They all tried to pretend that she was going to get better, that she was just having a bad day.

Henry went along with Audrey's wishes, but he had to ask Christine just one more time. Didn't she think they could keep her? It was important to him that they all stay together. It seemed wrong to give up one of his babies, and if he let them take her, it would be admitting that Audrey wasn't going to make it. And, dear God, she had to make it. What would they do without her?

Christine said, "No!, No!" She just couldn't handle one more. Enough was enough. No one bothered to really talk to Christine. No one asked how she was feeling. They couldn't understand all the anger. She felt betrayed and wondered if she would ever have a life of her own.

So as Audrey's youngest, Barbara's fate was sealed. When the news got out, others stepped forward and offered to take this one or that one. Belzie's sister Shelly and her husband offered to take Reba or Faye, but Henry was adamant. One was enough to part with. Just one and only one because it seemed to give Audrey peace of mind.

Then on Sunday morning, April 7, 1947, the hospital sent word that it was over. Henry, not knowing what to do, took all of his children and went to the hospital.

Walking down the corridor of the hospital, they were a strange sight. A very tall, strong looking man with tears rolling down his face, shaking with grief. Alongside him a young lady, Christine, carrying a small child, Faye in one arm and holding on to Reba with her other hand. Two very different looking children, to be from the same family, one so fair and blonde, the other a replica of the man. Behind the girl, three tall, young men, not old, maybe fifteen, fourteen and nine, Harvey, Dempsey, and Charles. And along the wall a ten-year-old, blonde, little girl who touched the wall as she walked saying, "It's not true, I know it's not true."

But it was true, Audrey Annell Dickinson White left the family she loved, her stay on this earth not nearly long enough...

Nobody out grows a-needin'
their momma.
Don't matter none how old
they are.

—Paralee White

CHAPTER THIRTY

The recovery, if indeed there was one, for those who loved Audrey, was a long and arduous one.

Henry, a young man by all standards with a very large family to provide for, was lost. His days and nights merged into one.

It became apparent to all that they could no longer stay in the house where Audrey's windows were such a prominent reminder of a much beloved wife and mother.

Faye, a toddler of three, searched for her mother continuously. Reba became much quieter, and Marie became an old ten-year-old child. Christine could not possibly fulfill all the roles she was expected to fulfill. The boys found excuses to stay away from home with this relative or that. They were a family in crisis. Billy was gone, and they did not have Audrey to tell them what to do next.

Paralee came for a visit. She left Will at home, enlisting Bud's services to drive her to Double Springs. She found the house spotless under Christine's supervision with the children all clean. What she had expected to find, she did not. They were a family in crisis, but they were a well organized family. Audrey's teachings were instilled in each child—order and cleanliness.

Henry simply could not function. He worked sporadically. He was angry with God and man. It was Henry that Paralee concentrated on. "It is time for you to come home," she told him.

Paralee was not speaking of her physical home but back to the area where he grew up. Paralee had long resented the fact Henry had moved to Winston County when he married Audrey. She felt he had deserted his family in favor of hers.

Henry, in no shape to argue with his mother, agreed they should move.

Barbara Jean was just down the road with Belzie and Olivet, and that fact made it hard to move; but Henry instructed Christine and

Marie to start packing. He was going to Walker County to find a job and a place for them to live, in that order. Not waiting to think his decision over, Henry left that very day with Paralee and Bud.

He was gone a week, returning only long enough to bring the children enough groceries for another week and instruct them to keep packing. He would be back for them on the following weekend.

Henry's choice of a new home was smaller than what they had, but it was closer to Bud and Vertie, Bart and Stella, and of course Paralee and Will. It was located in the small community of Thach, right in the middle of Walker County. The church and school were within walking distance.

Henry found a job working in the mines. He set up an account at the small store down the road for the children to obtain food and supplies. He was paid every two weeks, and on that Friday he would pay his grocery bill and the process would start all over again. He was still a hard worker, but his heart was not in it anymore. Many times he did not come home for two or three days at a time, leaving the children to fend for themselves. They never went hungry, but life was very hard for them.

Education was pretty much put on hold for Christine, who at seventeen was responsible for the younger children. The older boys came and went—hiring themselves out to local farmers, often spending a portion of their wages on clothes or toys for the little girls, Faye and Reba.

Just as aunts and uncles reared Audrey, other older members of their far-reaching families also guided her children. Harvey spent a lot of time with Wesley; Dempsey and Charles preferred Vertie and Bud's home.

They all checked on Barbara at every opportunity, often becoming a nuisance to Belzie and Olivet, who felt Barbara was their own child; yet she was theirs only on loan, and Henry might ask for her back at any time. Audrey had made it quite clear in her deathbed request: should Henry re-marry before Barbara was two, then Henry should be allowed to have her back in his home. They were afraid this would happen at any moment; every visit from Henry was critical in their eyes. He never asked, but when Barbara was five they decided to put some distance between her and her real family by moving to Indiana. But to soothe everyone's feelings, they promised they would bring her back to Alabama at least once a year for a visit. An only child with many sisters and brothers, Barbara grew up many miles and an entire culture away from her natural family.

Each child had a favorite aunt or cousin they liked to visit. Christine, on rare occasions would spend a few days with her friends, Opal and Mildred, Suz Hunter's daughters. Marie loved her Aunt Jean, taking every opportunity to go to her home for as long as Henry would let her stay.

Life settled into a routine for a little over two years, then Christine got married. She established her own home, but still had a foot in her old home, feeling responsible for the other children, often taking Reba with her. Marie had to grow older still, now she had to fill Christine's shoes, cooking and cleaning and keeping track of Charles and Faye. They were children rearing children.

Henry waited almost eight years before he re-married, marrying a widow with three boys. The marriage was an opening for Marie to get married and leave home, but the same marriage caused problems for Faye who had enjoyed many freedoms, having never had a mother, only a doting father, brothers, and sisters.

Audrey's true windows, her children grew into adults that she would have been very proud of, despite the tragedies that touched their lives.